FRESHMEN

F

Punch Line

Erin K. Butler

EPIC Press

Punch Line
Freshmen: Book #6

Written by Erin K. Butler

Published by EPIC Press™
PO Box 398166
Minneapolis, MN 55439

Printed in the United States of America.

Cover design by Kali VanZuilen
Images for cover art obtained from iStockPhoto.com
Edited by Kirsten Rue

LIBRARY OF CONGRESS CATALOGING-IN-PUBLICATION DATA

Names: Butler, Erin K., author.
Title: Punch line / by Erin K. Butler.
Description: Minneapolis, MN : EPIC Press, [2017] | Series: Freshmen
Summary: All her life, Kayla has played by her parents' rules, but everything changes when she arrives at Swimmer College in Boston. She starts to party and rebel against her old, strict upbringing, creating a new life for herself. But when she goes too far, she finds her whole college career at risk. As she makes and breaks friendships and grades, will she find a place for herself in college, or will she be forced to leave it all behind?
Identifiers: LCCN 2016931498 | ISBN 9781680763492 (lib. bdg.) | ISBN 9781680763355 (ebook)
Subjects: LCSH: College students—Fiction. | Identity—Fiction. | Interpersonal relations—Fiction. | Young adult fiction.
Classification: DDC [Fic]—dc23
LC record available at http://lccn.loc.gov/2016931498

EPIC Press

EPICPRESS.COM

For House Pemble,
for helping me through the year

CHAPTER 1

I had never seen so many pillows in one place. And I mean stupid pillows, like the kind that have peace signs and owls and aggressively geometric shapes all over them. The kind you wouldn't really put in your room after high school if you were the one making decisions. My mother picked one up from the top of the pile. It was bright pink and had neon-green cat ears—literally just the ears—printed in a pattern on the fabric.

"Oh, *Kayla*!" she said. "Look how cute!"

We were in Target, the college section. The one that markets almost exclusively to freshmen. As much as I secretly wanted ridiculous things to hang on my wall and too many storage bins, I had begun to change my mind when my mother started thinking the same way. I smiled thinly at her.

"I don't think I need throw pillows, Mom. I have a pillow for my bed already."

"What about for your couch?" she insisted.

"I don't have a couch. It's a dorm room."

"You can never have too many pillows."

"Actually, you can, though."

My mother frowned. "I just want you to be comfortable. Will you tell me if you need more pillows?"

"Yes, I'll tell you if I need more pillows," I said.

There were a dozen cans of soup in our shopping cart, most of which contained cheese in some form or other. Broccoli cheese. Tortilla cheese. Vegetable chicken multi-cheese. I figured I'd be good for a while in case I couldn't handle the dining hall. When I turned and she thought I couldn't see, my mother tossed one of the pillows on top of the cans.

School didn't start for a few weeks. My mother and I were shopping, though really, I had been shopping for months. Mostly, it was by myself, and I never bought anything. But I picked out my sheets, my posters, and the gilded-frame mirror that would hang on the back of my door. That was before I even knew who my roommate was, or if I would have one. It was the thing I did for myself, the one thing I could do to fight against the overwhelming disappointment of ending up at my second choice.

"I want you to feel comfortable there, Kayla. I want you to feel good."

My mother said these things to me a lot. Practically every day since I'd been accepted to Simmons. In a way, I thought, she had a point. She was right. I had never lived away from home, not even for summer camp. And that left parts of me feeling scared shitless. But, at the same time, wasn't living somewhere new just like living anywhere else? All sorts of people pulled off the living thing just fine in places that weren't New Jersey, where I had lived all my life. She couldn't have been as right as she thought she was.

And I definitely didn't need throw pillows for half a dorm room.

The roommate email had come the day before, on Friday afternoon. I'd been refreshing my inbox for days, and honestly almost peed when it finally came. I made myself wait a full ten seconds before opening it.

Dear KAYLA HOWARD,

. . . Clearly pulled from a list somewhere, they hadn't even changed the case . . .

The Office of Residential Life has assigned you the following roommate:

NAME: GRACE WILLEMS
GENDER: FEMALE
MAJOR: BIOCHEMISTRY

Your residential assignment for the 2015–2016 academic year is:

DORMITORY: BIGELOW HALL
ROOM: 211

Your roommate has been assigned based on the questionnaire you submitted earlier this summer. Your residential assignment has been chosen via a random lottery. We encourage you to contact your roommate before official move-in on September 1. Thank you, and we wish you all the best this year.

Sincerely,
SIMMONS COLLEGE
OFFICE OF RESIDENTIAL LIFE

Really, I had two main problems with this. One: why did they bother to specify Grace's gender? I knew I was going to an all-girls school. They knew it, too. So that was clearly just a cruel reminder. And, two: how was I supposed to contact this Grace? It's not like they gave me much information—not even enough to Facebook stalk, really.

It felt, in a way, like a disappointment. But it was the sort of disappointment I wanted. The sort of disappointment that, maybe, would finally convince my parents what a terrible idea Simmons was in the first place, which would mean they would let me wait a year and apply to other schools.

No such luck. I showed my mother the email when it came, and she immediately hopped onto Facebook and began frighteningly precise searches that combined "Grace Willems" with "Simmons College" and "class of 2019." A smiling girl in a track uniform popped up on the screen in less than a minute.

My mother was embarrassingly adept at Facebook.

She stood over my shoulder and watched as I sent Grace a friend request, then typed out a message that boiled down to: *Hi! I'm your new roommate!* Part of me was angry that she made me do it, but a louder part didn't know what I would have done otherwise.

Grace messaged me back an hour later. Now, on Saturday, my mother and I were in Target, and we were buying a fridge that we (the three of us) had collectively decided I would bring. Move-in day was in less than a month.

"I was thinking, why don't you invite Annie and Liz over this weekend?" my father asked two weeks later.

Silence. I pushed the food around on my plate. Spaghetti, as if my parents had known I would need a food good for pushing, and so they gave me the most pushable. My father continued as if I had answered.

"You could make a whole weekend out of it. I can drive you girls to the movies tomorrow night, and they can stay overnight. We'll leave you alone."

“I have my license, you know,” I said.

“Right,” he nodded. “Yeah. So you could even drive.”

“That would be a nice idea, before you all go off to school,” my mother added. I didn’t look at either of them. I didn’t say, sure, I would love to spend my last weekend at home with a bunch of girls, right before I move in with a bunch of girls, and only girls, for the next four years. I didn’t say that I had skipped all the graduation parties, all of them, because I knew the sort of things they would do there, and I knew my parents wouldn’t have approved. Not that they would have known, anyway. And yet, spending my last weekend with the same girls I had always known seemed like a cruel caricature of myself.

It wasn’t that I didn’t love Annie and Liz. I did. They were my best friends, and had been on my same wavelength all through high school. The most alcohol they had ever had was what they accidentally swallowed in mouthwash. But that was exactly the point. With them, with Simmons—was this what I would be forever?

Somehow, before I could say, *No, absolutely not,* my head was nodding at my parents' expectant faces. Their eyes were bright, as if they were children, and my mind flashed back to the day I had gotten my acceptance letter. They had watched over my shoulder as I slid my finger under the envelope's flap and pulled out the dense packet covered with smiling girls' faces. *Kayla, we are so proud of you. Kayla, this is what you've been waiting for.* As if I hadn't been waiting for Georgetown's letter the day before, with the thin *No* hiding on its underbelly. Simmons suddenly crept its way to the forefront and became the only option—the silent killer.

"I'll call Annie and Liz," I heard myself say.

Liz sighed as soon I invited them. The three of us were on the phone that night, and I could almost feel the heave of Liz's breath through the speaker.

"Seriously? A movie and a sleepover? It's our last weekend, guys," she said.

"Plus, I have plans with Dan," Annie added.

"Yeah, and I have plans with whoever I meet at the seniors' party on Saturday," Liz said.

"You know we're not seniors anymore, right?" I chimed in. "Like, we graduated. That's not a thing."

"Whatever, there's still a party on Saturday before everyone leaves. And I'm actually going to go."

"Oh, stop it, you are not," I said.

"It's our last chance. I'm not about to doom my reputation in this town forever."

"What reputation?"

"Actually, Dan and I were thinking of going, too," Annie said.

"But you and Dan will be together next year. You guys can't leave me alone for our last weekend." I was starting to panic a little bit.

"The same way you can't let me get through all of high school without going to a real party," Liz said.

"You've kind of already done that," Annie told her.

"Shut up."

"Listen," I cut in, "this is our last chance to do something like this together for a while. Until Christmas break, anyway." Liz sighed once more for effect.

"Fine, if it's that important to you," she conceded.

"I guess Dan and I can reschedule," Annie said.

"Thanks, guys. Really. It'll make me feel better." And my parents, too, I didn't add.

Annie and Liz showed up together the next night, ringing the doorbell around dinnertime. Annie had driven them both in her boyfriend Dan's old jeep. I raised my eyebrows at her when she came in.

"You're driving his car now?" I asked.

"Seriously, you guys are so married, I can't handle it," Liz said. She crossed her eyes and feigned gagging. Annie just shrugged.

"At least I'll know someone where I'm going," she answered.

They followed me into the living room, where I had already put out a big bowl of popcorn and set up the TV. Being a little too mortified to go out to a place that was not the "senior class" party, I had decided that we would decline my dad's offer and spend the night in with *Gilmore Girls*. My dad even ordered us a pizza, as if aware of the sacrifices we wholesome girls were making.

As Carole King started singing the theme song we all knew by heart, we took our usual places: me in the big armchair, Annie on the couch, and Liz on the floor with her back up against it. Annie and Liz were each absently, separately, hugging their knees to their chest.

"What if everyone has a Dan, though?" Liz said before we had even finished singing along.

"You mean what if you're single forever?" I joked.

"Not kidding, dipshit. I mean, like, what if

everybody at Penn knows somebody already, so I have no way of getting an in?"

"That's ridiculous," I said. "People go to Penn from literally all over the world. No way does everyone have someone they know already."

"All they need to know is one person," Liz insisted. "Then that person introduces them to all their new friends, and vice versa, and then there is this whole network of freshmen where I'm not included."

"I think you're missing the point. Where do all these new friends come from if people aren't going out meeting them?"

"Plus, you'll have a roommate, won't you?" Annie added. "See, you're actually the lucky one here. You get to start fresh. I'm already tied to Dan's people at Rutgers."

"Dan doesn't have any people," Liz pointed out.

"Exactly, but he will, and you will, too," Annie replied. "Except I won't, because I'm the weird girl who's already practically married."

"At least you guys will have options," I said. "I'll just have girls exclusively. These are girls who chose to actually, in the twenty-first century, spend their college years in a school that only lets in one gender. Who even are these people?"

"Well, you are one of them," Annie pointed out. She had taken a fistful of popcorn and was licking the salt off individual pieces before popping them in her mouth. "It could be that they're all in your same boat."

"I only applied to make my parents happy. I didn't realize it would end up being my only choice!"

"So you'll be in a school filled with a bunch of little Kaylas, all trying to please their parents. What a party." Liz smirked and fixed her eyes on the TV.

"I don't know what their deal is, that's the whole problem," I said, not ready to give up the spotlight to Rory Gilmore just yet. "I feel like this whole thing is doomed."

"What," Liz asked, "college?"

"No, I don't think so. This year, I guess. Freshman year is supposed to make or break you, isn't it?"

"Sure, in terms of your social life. I think for academic stuff, you've got a little more time to figure it out."

"But what if you guys make the social life thing work and we all come back and we're not friends anymore? You can't leave me alone with just Dan," Annie said. There was genuine fear in her eyes, as if she could already see a lifetime of tailgate weekends where she was the friendless wife who served the chips.

I tossed a pillow at her—taking a moment to reconsider my mother's stance on throw pillows—and grinned. "After you guys ditched everything to come hang out with me on your last weekend as pre-freshmen? I'm not too worried."

The next afternoon, I sat on my bed, finally preparing to start the daunting task of packing up my room. There was an overwhelming amount of work to do, and I had spent the last few weeks convincing myself that it was foolish to start early, since I was still living there and would need whatever was in my room—literally all of it, including my winter clothes. Now, with just days to go, I couldn't put it off any longer.

I started with my clothes, which really meant picking out the clothes I would wear for the next few days. Everything else would get packed. Picking out my final outfits felt like a time bomb. Each top was a *tick, tick, tick* that counted ominously down to the one-way trip to Boston. I tried to combat it with extra accessories—accent scarves in summertime—until I reached the limited amount that my last suitcase would hold.

Next came my desk. I emptied its contents into a cardboard box, not bothering to reorganize. The top barely closed. I secretly hoped that having a laptop would mean I'd never have to use things like pencils and highlighters again, but that was not a risk I was willing to take just yet.

After that, I transferred the contents of Target bags to bigger boxes. It was a little astounding how much stuff my mother and I had figured it would take to keep me alive in college. Between sheets, bars of soap, desk lamps, paper trays, coffee mugs, and towels, I wondered how we would ever fit everything in the car. I filled three boxes by the time the bags were empty. Then, I rolled up all my clothes—a tip two separate classmates had offered—and filled my suitcases.

The last thing to pack up was the little table beside my bed. This was the one I'd been avoiding. The table served many purposes, some more important than others. On top, I had a pile of scattered receipts and loose change, plus my corsage from prom that I had been drying out since May. There was also *The Catcher in the Rye*, which I was reading for the second time, with a bookmark halfway through. Beneath the surface, though, in the drawers, I kept the things that were most important to bring with me.

A graduation pamphlet. Ticket stubs from *The Lion King*. A photo of Liz, Annie, and me at Springfest. Another photo, this one framed, of my parents and me. An unsmoked cigarette someone had given me at the homecoming pep rally my senior year. The Valentines that Liz and Annie and I had exchanged each year since the sixth grade. A heart-shaped necklace from my one and only tenth-grade boyfriend, its chain tangled in two spots.

I climbed up on my chair and reached to the top of my closet, where there was an empty box shaped like a high-heeled shoe. It had come from an aunt years ago for a birthday. I don't think I had ever opened it, and I had to blow dust off the lid. Carefully, I placed each object inside, then taped it shut.

Tuesday morning, early, we loaded up the car.

My dad insisted on carrying most of the heavy things, which I simultaneously appreciated and found irritating. We were ready to go by eight thirty. All the way to Boston, my mother alternated between crying and singing along with the radio.

CHAPTER 2

Bigelow Hall was not as big as I expected it to be. Part of it, I think, was that I had been saying the words over and over in my head for so long that I'd gotten fixated on the "big" part of the name. In reality, it was a four-floor building filled end-to-end with double-rooms. Grace was already in 211 when I got there, with the door wide open to greet me.

"Hey! Hi!" she called out when I knocked. She jumped off the bare mattress where she had been sitting and contemplating her stack of boxes. "I'm Grace."

"This is Kayla," my dad said. *Sheesh. Glad to know I could handle my first introduction.*

"Hi. I'm Kayla," I cut in, then stuck out my hand to shake. Grace laughed and went in for a hug. Her body was warm and firm and unexpected. When we moved apart, I asked, "Did your parents leave already?"

Grace laughed again. "They couldn't make the trek from California," she said. Which I should have known, and which I was jealous of. The being-from-California part and the chance to start all of this alone with a clean slate.

"Right. Of course."

"We would be happy to help out if you need anything!" my mother chimed in. I glared at her, worried that she would usurp my roommate before I had any say in the matter.

"Thanks, that's so nice of you!" Grace said. "I think I've just got to unpack everything, and I'll be all set." She was so incredibly in control.

So we got to unpacking, too. First the car, then my boxes and suitcases. The entire residence campus was a nightmare. Everyone was stressed out, which just made everyone around them more stressed. Plus, Bigelow Hall didn't have an elevator, which meant that the building was quickly filled with sweaty, cranky eighteen-year-old girls and their parents. No one had any desire to meet their new dorm-mates or even offer any sort of greeting. It was worse than I could have imagined it would be.

Boston was so hot that afternoon that my shirt was soon soaked through with sweat. For the first time since being accepted to Simmons, I was glad there were no boys. It was slightly less mortifying to be sweating my eyeballs out when I was surrounded by other girls experiencing the same thing. But only slightly.

When the biggest boxes had been unpacked and I was reasonably settled, my parents began to look around the room and gather their things. For the first time, it hit me that they would drive home and we would go to bed in separate places, and in the morning, wake up there, too. My mom wouldn't poke her head through my bedroom door to wake me up—who would make sure I got up on time? My dad wouldn't make me toast with too much butter. And when I got ready to go to class, I wouldn't be going to the high school, I'd be going to a building I had never seen before. It was tragic and delicious and overwhelming, and I felt everything all at once.

"Don't cry! Don't miss us too much!" my mother said, though her own eyes were already wet. She smothered me in a hug. My dad came over and joined, awkwardly draping his arm over the both of us. Grace watched silently from her bed.

"Kayla hates getting up in the morning. Give her a nudge, would you?" my mother said to Grace as she pulled away.

"*Mom.*"

"You'll call us if you need anything," my dad said. It was a statement, not a question.

"You'll call us every day!" my mother cried.

"I'll call you."

Then they turned toward the door and gave me one last look. And they were gone.

I stared at the closed door for a few moments after they left. “Sorry,” I said to Grace. “They can be a little overbearing sometimes.”

“They’re sweet!” Grace smiled, then jumped off the freshly made bed and smoothed the corners. “Mind if I prop the door open? I’ve heard it’s the best way to meet people.”

“Sure.”

Grace was tall and lean, and I wondered briefly if she would fit on the bed, even though it was an extra-long twin. Her hair was thick and dark and hung all the way down her back, even tied up, as it was, in a ponytail. She had replaced the track uniform from her Facebook picture with a Simmons College Track T-shirt. It had all the freshmen’s names listed on the back. Her name was already on a T-shirt. We had been at school for less than three hours.

"So, you're already on the track team?" I said. "How did you manage that?"

"Recruiting," Grace said matter-of-factly, as though it made no difference to her that she already had a place carved out and defined for her on campus. "We had practice already, this morning. Can you believe that?"

"That's crazy. How did you manage that with move-in?" I asked.

"A little bit of one thing followed by a little bit of the other. I didn't peg this for a fun day. From what I hear, that's just what they do to the freshmen."

Who had she heard this from? How was she already getting insider information when we had just gotten to Boston?

"So, what's your thing?" she continued.

I stared at her blankly. "My thing? What do you mean?"

"What do you do? What's your major? What are your classes?"

"Um, I'm mostly taking gen eds. I haven't declared yet."

"Oh, me either, officially," Grace said, and I felt better for a moment. Then she added, "But I'm probably doing biochemistry." Well, there went that. "That's so awesome, though, that you haven't declared yet. It leaves everything so open," she continued.

"Yeah. The world is my oyster, or something." *Or something.* The thing was, I wasn't even mad or specifically jealous. Grace was so sincere and warm about it all. It was seductively easy to like her immediately.

Just then, a head peeped in our room, followed by two afterthought raps on the door.

"Anybody home?"

We clearly were.

"Hey! I'm Grace." She stuck out her hand to shake.

"I'm Christina. Nice to meet you. How's the move-in?"

"You know." Grace gestured to the messy room, to the yet-unpacked boxes. "About what you'd expect. I'm sure you're in the same boat."

I was in the awkward position of now being part of the conversation without ever having introduced myself.

"Oh, yeah. My roommate Shruti and I have been unpacking for hours, and our room is still a total disaster area."

"Yeah," I said. *A-plus contribution, Kayla.*

"Are you guys going to the Freshmen Welcome?" Christina asked. She seemed mechanically excited—the sort of excited that you talk yourself into beforehand—and a little nervous. As she threw questions at us, she alternated between twisting her fingers together and pushing her shoulder-length hair behind her ear.

"I was planning to. What about you, Kayla?" Grace said. I was really quite impressed with how she worked my name in without making anyone feel uncomfortable.

"It's required, isn't it? I was planning on it, too."

"Great!" Christina said. "Shruti and I and a few girls from the hall are heading over in a few minutes. Want to join?"

"Sounds great," Grace answered.

We grabbed our freshly pressed IDs and waited in the hallway for Shruti and the other girls on our floor. Shruti appeared from the room next door in a few moments, followed by two other girls. They were all impossibly beautiful, with short, flattering skirts. Two girls had pixie cuts; another had long, glossy hair that flowed all down her back. One of the girls had a line of earrings that went all the way up one ear.

"Hey! Are we neighbors?" Shruti asked.

"Yup! This is Grace and Kayla," Christina answered for Grace and me. We nodded.

"Awesome," Shruti said. "So we're all hall-mates." She gestured to the two girls with her. We all grinned a little stupidly at one another. It was pretty artificial, I thought, and maybe even a little cruel, to meet people this way. We'd all been thrust into this situation, this more-or-less home with one another, and we were expected already to be some sort of something together. Clearly, some of them were. Shruti and her glamorous friends seemed to have done it. Was this the sort of freshmen clique that Liz had been worrying about? Liz and Annie flashed suddenly across my mind, and I imagined them waltzing through their own move-in days and promptly replacing me. Meanwhile, I hadn't even figured out where the shower was to wash off my move-in-sweaty body.

At this point, though, there was no time for that. The six of us made our way, gaggle-like, down the stairs and out the doors of Bigelow. Shruti, who already seemed to know her way around, led us down Park Drive to the academic campus. There was an enormous tent set up on the green. It even had doors that looked like they were made out of plastic wrap. We went inside and took seats safely in the middle of a row.

Looking around me, there were only girls. Girls literally everywhere. It felt a little bit like a horror movie, or a story I had read once about a tribe of women who lived on an island and had banished all men, forever. It was completely surreal.

"A little spooky, isn't it?" Grace leaned over and whispered to me, clearly noticing the same thing. "I've never been to an all-girls school."

"Then how did you end up here?" I asked her.

"Circumstances. You know," she said. "When they recruited me, it was the best option, and so here I am. Was it like that for you, too?"

Grace was looking at me expectantly, waiting for my answer as if it held the key to normalcy. It was funny; I hadn't seen a sliver of doubt in her until then. Yet even she was sitting here in this foreign place nursing insecurities. But then I remembered that I hadn't been recruited for anything, I was just *here*—it wasn't my best option, it was my only one.

"Yeah, it was definitely circumstantial," I told her. "Not exactly what I was hoping for."

"It's been nice so far, though, hasn't it? I mean, the parts of Boston I've seen so far are beautiful."

I perked up at this—Boston really *was* beautiful, as I noticed when my parents and I drove through the city, but I hadn't given conscious thought to it until then. But it was true. The Charles River wound serenely through the city; ancient trees lined parks and sidewalks; and a handful of downtown buildings towered and gleamed in the sunlight. "Absolutely," I said, and I smiled for maybe the first time that day.

The tent was loud around us as freshmen girls tried somewhat frantically to make new friends. Up at the front of the tent was a podium and a screen that had the Simmons College logo and mascot (an aggressive cartoon shark) projected onto it. A woman stepped up to the podium and cleared her throat into the microphone, and the tent fell silent.

"To the class of 2019," she began, "Welcome. My name is Elaine Storey, and I am the Dean of Simmons College. Many of you are probably overwhelmed by this city, by Simmons, and by moving in. I assure you that this is perfectly normal, and that things will settle down quickly. You'll feel as if you've always been here . . . "

As Dean Storey continued her welcome speech, my thoughts trailed off in the hazy pool of her words. She seemed to be saying a lot of nothing over and over again, and the repetition lulled me into the sort of trance where I could breathe for the first time all day. When I looked at the girls around me, I saw that many of them had glazed-over eyes, too. I wondered if anyone would even remember our welcome.

I didn't know how long she spoke for, but at some point, the girls started clapping. Before long, a group of RAs who were inexplicably energetic were herding us into groups for campus tours. I stayed self-protectively with the group from my floor.

Simmons in the late-summer twilight was like a postcard. Our enthusiastic RA was pointing out important things like classrooms and the library and the cafeteria, but I was too distracted by the scenery to remember much of anything. The sun set over massive buildings that mixed the historical with modern, sleek architecture. As we walked through buildings and in and out inconspicuous doors, my eyes drank in everything.

If I was being honest, I hadn't expected Simmons to be beautiful. In my mind, it was too closely linked to my great collegiate failure; my inability to get myself to a place where I could be someone different. It seemed impossible that a place so representative of my stunted life could be beautiful. Yet as I toured the campus that night, small though it was with just a handful of buildings, I felt wrapped in the comfort of its embrace.

The RA led us back down the road to the residential campus, where she brought us to the second floor lounge of Bigelow. We all sat on nouveau-psychedelic couches and beanbag chairs that were placed geometrically around a carpet.

"Hey, guys," she said. "So, as you just heard at Welcome, my name is Claudia, and I'm your RA this year. I'm a junior, and my major is Poli Sci. First things first: my door is always open. If you want to chat, whether it's about Bigelow or classes or anything, just knock. Second things second: don't let D. Sto bring you down. Her whole schtick is not what Simmons is about."

D. Sto? I had no idea what she was talking about. Claudia must have seen the puzzled looks on our faces, because she grinned and continued, "D. Sto is what we call the dean, Dean Storey. We really like nicknames here. So, on that note, let's introduce ourselves."

Here we go, I thought. What would it be? Name game? Human knot? My-name-is-Kayla-I-brought-kiwis?

"Tell us your name, where you're from, your major if you have it, and the thing that scares you most about college," Claudia instructed.

Well, that got personal pretty fast.

"Anyone want to go first?"

"I'll go," said Grace, raising her hand. Though I

wasn't particularly surprised, I was impressed. "My name is Grace, and I'm from California. I'm majoring in biochemistry. I'd say I'm probably most afraid of winter in Boston. How do y'all manage it?"

Everyone giggled at that, and we all felt a little less tense.

Shruti, sitting next to Grace, went next. "I'm Shruti, and I'm from Connecticut. I'm majoring in communications, and I can't honestly say I'm afraid of anything here. I've been waiting to come to Simmons for ages."

My turn was next. I took a deep breath and swallowed audibly. "Hi, I'm Kayla, and I'm from New Jersey," I said. "I, um, am not really sure what to major in yet. And I'm afraid of not figuring it out, like, ever. Or not figuring out what I want to do with maybe my whole life or even what clubs to join here or whatever. Which kind of makes me panic?" The words sort of slipped out, in that I blurted them, and I bit my lip when I was finished. I had either been the girl who said what everyone was thinking, or the girl who said what no one was thinking, and either way, I had made it awkward. Everyone looked at me a little uncomfortably, and then the girl sitting next to me picked up the introductions again.

That night, all the girls on my floor, including our RA, ordered pizza and watched *The Princess Bride* in the cozy lounge. It was a relaxed, slumber party-type night, but I was so embarrassed about my spaz attack that I shut my mouth and kept to myself. No one except Grace spoke to me, but a few girls gave me sympathetic looks that made me think they pitied me a little. Grace, mercifully, did impressions as she recited lines along with the movie, and that, at least, made me laugh. When I was ready for bed, my first time sharing a room with another person, I wiggled into my nightgown in the closet and slept on top of the sheets.

The next day was a combination orientation and first day of classes. Going into it felt like eating a taco salad where you only knew what some of the ingredients were: it was definitely risky and could possibly make you sick. However, I didn't have much of a choice except to take a bite.

I woke up to Grace's alarm clock in the morning. She was already up, and she smiled at me as I climbed out of bed. The bed rose higher off the floor than I was used to, and I stumbled a little. Grace laughed.

"It's weird adjusting to a new bed, isn't it?" she said. I grinned.

"Not as weird as the 'mawwiage' guy, I guess," I replied, referencing the priest in *The Princess Bride* from the night before.

"I'll give you ten bucks if you talk like that all day," she said, and I grinned again.

"Are you doing orientation this morning?" I asked.

"Yup! Let's walk down together," she answered.

We met up with our group from the night before and headed to the academic campus.

The quad was once again swarming with eager freshmen, all split into cliques for their imagined safety. A plump, friendly-looking woman blew a whistle, and space cleared around her in the center of the quad. She started speaking to us through a megaphone.

"Good morning, girls!" she called. "I hate to use this thing." She waved the megaphone, distorting her voice. "But there are an awful lot of you, and I want you all to hear. Now, as you know from your welcome packets, classes begin this afternoon. But first, we will finish your orientation. That means getting to know Boston. Simmons might just be the buildings you see here, but the whole city is your campus. Make sure you've got someone to stick with, and let's start our tour!"

I wished that I had paid a little more attention to the orientation schedule. In reality, I had spent so much time being angry about Simmons that I hadn't bothered to study schedules or plans for the first few days.

I followed along as we trudged as a herd through the city. It was a whirlwind—between Fenway Park, the Common, and riding the T, I felt like I could barely breathe after seeing even a fraction of the city. Yet it was thrilling. All morning, I was so distracted that I didn't speak to a single girl in my class, but I hungrily took in all the parts of Boston that danced around me. I could picture myself in the city for years; I could walk for miles and miles. It was too soon when we headed back to campus for the first classes of the day.

But, back on campus, there was yet another surprise. As we entered the gates to disperse into various buildings and classrooms, I looked at the students scurrying along on their way, and I saw—*men*. I stopped in my tracks, and my eyes grew wide.

"Is this—isn't this an all-girls school?" I asked, incredulous.

Shruti, standing beside me, laughed. "For

undergrad, yeah. There's a whole graduate school for anyone, though. Didn't you know?"

There was a bit of an edge in her voice, but I barely minded. In less than a day, Simmons had gone from being something I detested to a place full of possibilities I wouldn't mind uncovering. I laughed amiably back at Shruti, then turned toward my class building without saying another word.

My first class, Principles of Education, was surprisingly easy to find. I glanced hesitantly around the room and then took a seat, a little unnerved by the concept of non-assigned seating. A few seats away, I spotted a girl from our Boston tour, and she waved.

The professor, when she came in, was somehow deceptively small-looking, even though she was of average height. She wore a jacket that my dad would have described as a sport coat—and that he would have disapproved of a woman wearing—with leathery patches on the elbows, and a wide, woolen skirt that seemed to scoff at the heat. After smiling briefly at us, she put her bag down on the desk and pawed at the console that powered the projector.

"This is the first class for some of you, yes?" she asked. We glanced at one another, the classroom almost full, and most of us nodded. "Welcome, then," she continued, "to Simmons. My name is Dottie Lloyd, and I will be teaching Principles of Education this semester."

Dottie Lloyd, seriously? This did not bode well. I couldn't legitimately take a professor seriously if her name was Dottie. Plus, being a professor meant she had probably gotten a Ph.D. So what did her degree say? Dr. Dottie? Dottie, Ph.D.? I began to expect the ridiculous and faltered a little in my newfound hope.

"You will call me Dr. Lloyd," she added. The Dottie business was immediately out the window. She made it clear with the force of her expression that we were not allowed to bullshit this class.

The projector turned on, and a slideshow flickered to life on the screen. I opened up my computer, fresh for note-taking, while Dr. Lloyd passed out a syllabus.

Syllabi were new to me, and a little bit fascinating. Here was the entire semester laid out before me, everything I would need to know and be responsible for. It was at the same time overwhelming and strangely comforting.

Dr. Lloyd made her way back to the podium up front and instantly regained command of the room. The slideshow behind her flashed pictures of sharp pencils, testing booklets, and dusty chalkboards.

"Take a look at these items," Dr. Lloyd said, pointing to the screen. "What do these have in common?"

A girl in the front row, a pin-straight blonde with blue eyes, raised her hand. "They're all, um, school stuff," she said. She was serious. Dr. Lloyd blinked.

"Anyone else?"

"They probably cost more than a teacher's budget," another girl called out, and the girls around her giggled. But I looked at the pictures and suddenly knew what Dr. Lloyd meant. I raised my hand.

"They're all outdated," I said. "Everything there—nothing up there is going to cut it in a classroom today. Do kids even use chalk anymore? I think we need to change with the times, and do things differently if the way we teach is going to work."

Dr. Lloyd smiled, and I felt a flush of unexpected pride.

"Exactly," she said. "The study of education is about being innovative and bringing new ideas forward. A teacher's mind should be broadening just as much as their students' minds. Some of you, I know, may be here to fulfill a requirement. But let me assure you, the principles you will learn in this class are ones you can apply everywhere. This semester, I want you to put aside what you know and what is comfortable, and dive into concepts you've never considered before. So, let's begin."

To my utter surprise, I found my lips stretched into a smile that matched Dr. Lloyd's. I sat up straight in my chair and readied my fingers to type.

CHAPTER 3

Classes picked up in a blur, in a frenzy, in everything I had never had in high school. Between Principles of Ed, Psych, Econ, Music Theory, and Calc, I found myself swept into a regular, if somewhat hectic, routine. Classes filled my mornings, and I spent afternoons exploring first the campus, and then other neighborhoods around Boston. Evenings were spent with Grace and Christina, our neighbor, in the dining hall. The three of us hunkered down in the library after that for homework. It was a little isolated, but it was soothing. Grace and Christina reminded me of Liz and Annie—Grace for her vivaciousness, Christina for the nervous but kind way about her. The familiarity was so comforting that I almost didn't mind the eerie similarity to my same old life.

Often, before dinner, I called my parents in New Jersey. My mother always picked up after the first ring, so I took to calling at the same time every day so that she wouldn't sit around waiting. After a few weeks, I even found myself missing them a bit. It wasn't as satisfying to procrastinate on my homework when there was no one pestering me to do it.

But if I was being honest, Simmons was much better than I had expected. It was peaceful. I found myself actually enjoying waking up in the morning—later than I'd had to wake up for high school—and walking through fall's morning mist to the academic campus. There were always giant Canada geese on the path, and when I wasn't busy watching out for goose poop, I closed my eyes and basked in the strangeness of being in city-nature.

Plus, Grace turned out to be the perfect roommate for me. She was quiet and tidy, and since she woke up early for track practice, she kept me on schedule. Sometimes, before we fell asleep, we would turn off the lights and look at the glow-in-the-dark stars we had stuck to the ceiling and just talk. She would tell me about the track team and her experience in high school as the only girl in the advanced chemistry classes. I would talk about Annie and Liz and the way we had been in high school, the dependable if bland weekends we used to spend together.

Grace, though, was better at making friends than I was. She seemed to have people in every one of her classes. I, on the other hand, couldn't seem to talk to anyone in class. What was I supposed to say to a stranger? Hi, I'm Kayla, and I'm in the market for a friend? I kept to myself, and even when we had to talk in groups or partners, the girls were always no more than cordial toward me. They had already formed their tight little squads, and I had missed the boat, without a plan for rescue in sight. I at least met some of Grace's friends, though, when she brought them to the library for our study sessions.

In our trio, Christina seemed to be having the same problem as I was. While at least I had Grace, Christina's roommate, Shruti, had almost immediately dropped her in favor of a well-dressed, unsmiling group of girls from our floor and the neighboring dorm. Even in the orchestra, where Christina played the flute, everyone seemed to be either aggressively serious about their music or already friends. She fell into the habit of coming back to Bigelow looking glum, and then heading silently to the library with us.

I was a little confused about how it had happened. After all, I wasn't *unfriendly*. Neither was Christina. We were just quiet. And I didn't have orchestra. Or track. Or debate, or intramural, or student government. In fact, I wasn't quite sure how people went about getting into these things. Had everyone else come to college with some instruction manual I didn't get?

The nice thing was that Grace, Christina, and I had each other on the weekends when the work let up. On weekends, I stopped worrying about Calc and the piles of reading I had to do, and the three of us watched movies and explored the city together. Group walks were different than the solo walks I took in the afternoon, but gratifying in their own way. They were comfortable companionship, and they brought me to the places that stuck out to Grace and Christina, where I wouldn't have gone on my own. It didn't take long to fall into a pleasant normalcy, just as Dean Storey—or D. Sto—had predicted.

Columbus Day weekend arrived before I was fully aware any time had passed. It was our very first long weekend in college.

My mother had called me the Wednesday before, preempting my evening call. "Are you coming home this weekend?" she asked as soon as I had said hello.

"Coming home? It's just a weekend, Mom."

"A long weekend! You have Monday off. We do, too."

"It's kind of a long way to go just for a few days. Plus, I have my first midterms next week." It wasn't a lie. If I had any prayer for Calc, I'd need to spend most of the weekend redoing my problem sets. Mostly, though, I was looking forward to an entire long weekend in Boston. The leaves had turned and were drifting deliciously all over the city, and I had plans with Grace and Christina to go to the Public Gardens and the Common.

"I'll help you study," my mother said.

Was she serious? "I don't think that will help. I really think I should stay here."

My mother sighed. "Well," she said, "you know best what you need for your classes."

"Thanks. I'm sorry, though."

"It's okay, I understand." She paused. "Kayla?"

"Yeah?"

"I miss you."

My throat got tight and I frowned as I heard the strain in her voice. To my surprise, my bottom lip began to tremble. "I miss you too, Mom," I said, meaning it, despite everything.

Friday evening after my last class felt like a blessed relief. Professors had let up on other assignments and readings to let us focus on midterms, and maybe even enjoy the long weekend a little. Leslie Leopold, respected scholar in the field of child psychology (a fact she made sure we remembered) and professor of my last Friday afternoon class, spent the last part of class going over how we could, if we so chose, use the scientific method to determine whether we had enjoyed the weekend once it was over. I fell into exhausted sleep embarrassingly soon after dinner.

In the morning, Grace, Christina, and I hopped on the Green Line to get to the Public Gardens. We got off at Arlington and made our way up the stairs. With the still-temperate weather, the Gardens were swamped with people, both locals and tourists.

"Which one do you think we count as," Christina asked, "locals or tourists?"

"Well, we're not really sightseeing," I pointed out.

"But we don't live here, not really," Grace said.

It was an interesting if slightly unnerving question, and I thought about it as we walked through the Gardens. In lots of ways, I felt like a visitor. Strolling among the flowers and trees made me feel like a Victorian lady caught in time. Yet I also felt distinctly at home and could scarcely imagine another place I'd rather be.

Grace took pictures of the trees in their semi-naked state, and I felt embarrassed for their vulnerability. Christina posed in a few of the pictures, clutching fall blossoms she had plucked from the ground, and leaning back dramatically. Grace and I laughed and made her promise to post the pictures online.

After the Gardens, we wandered over to the Common. It was huge and bustling with people, even more than the Gardens.

"Oh my gosh, this is the cutest thing I've ever seen," Christina said. She squealed, childlike, and pointed to the swan boats on the little pond. We grinned and crossed a majestic bridge, as if out of a fairy tale, over the pond.

"Can we just sit for a couple minutes?" Grace asked, and so we settled on the banks of the pond. It really was gorgeous. From our spot on the grass, we could see the golden dome of the Old State House reaching into the sky; we could hear music from a violinist who had taken up a spot on the path; we could watch children chase squirrels, screaming with glee. It didn't seem real; it seemed too nice. All at once, I felt the city rushing around me, and I tried helplessly to fit myself into its context.

Then, walking from the other side of the park, I saw Shruti and her flock of girls making their way down the path. They were six abreast and took up the entire width of the path. Each of the girls held shopping bags, and they were talking loudly over one another.

It was soon after I saw them that Shruti spotted the three of us on the bank. She didn't say anything, but she nudged the girl beside her. I recognized the girl from my Econ class; she spoke often and irrelevantly. Shruti and the girl started to laugh, and soon, the rest of the girls erupted into laughter, too, as the giggle passed down the line like the wave at a baseball game.

They laughed all the way down the path until they reached us, and then kept laughing. They didn't say a single word the whole time.

Christina watched them with a combination of fear and hurt in her eyes. One of the girls, a little plainer than the others, gave us a vaguely apologetic look, but Christina just scowled. Grace sighed and looked tired by it all.

I wished they had said something, anything at all. The fact that they could laugh without words meant they'd spent enough time talking about us already—we were an established joke. Sure, our trio was small and tame and quiet, all things considered. But I hadn't realized how completely that set us apart from everyone else.

"Let's go back," I said, standing up abruptly. I expected protest, but none came. Grace and Christina gathered their things and stood up to follow me.

The Green Line was full for the first train back to Simmons. We made it onto the second train, but we all stood, because a middle-aged man in a suit had spread his bags over an entire row of seats.

Christina disappeared into her room for the rest of the afternoon. I sat in my room and tried to concentrate on studying, mostly unsuccessfully, while Grace Skyped with some of her friends back home. Finally, she turned off her computer. I shut my notebook and suggested that we get dinner. Really, I just ate a lot of fries.

When Grace and I got back from the dining

hall, we had just plugged in Netflix for the night when someone knocked on our door. We glanced at one another, and Grace hopped up to answer it. Standing outside was Shruti, her glossy hair flowing behind her, hanging well past her short skirt.

"Hey, guys! We're going to a party off campus. Want to come?" she said. Grace was smiling politely, but even from where I was sitting, I could smell the vodka practically radiating off Shruti. She had never been so pleasant to us. Suddenly, she leaned in toward Grace and gave us both a knowing look. "Just to let you know," she added, "there will be alcohol."

That is when I knew what she was doing. Here we were, the athlete and her less glamorous roommate, in our room on a Saturday night and about to watch *The Office*. Two girls who lived in a substance-free room. Two freshmen who had never made it outside the dorm to a party or even been invited. One girl who kept on being what she had always been.

Grace, whose smile had turned into one of grandmotherly pity, was opening her mouth to thank Shruti and send her off when something inside me broke and I spoke up.

"All set with your TV now, Grace?" I said, and turned to face Shruti. I narrowed my eyes and took on a serious look as the decision solidified itself and took hold. "I was just about to go out." Shruti and Grace both looked surprised at first. Then, Shruti glanced over my sweats and smirked. "After I change, I mean," I added. I kept my eyes on the ground as I fished through my closet for a top I had bought just after orientation. It still had the tags attached.

I ripped them off and wiggled out of my tank top, feeling momentarily bold enough to be in just my bra in front of Grace and Shruti. The new shirt stretched tight over my chest, and the first thing I thought when I looked down was that I looked bulbous. That was really the word that came to mind, *bulbous*. I shrugged it away and slipped on a pair of skinny jeans. "Let's go," I said. Grace had already pressed play on *The Office*. Shruti stumbled once against the doorframe before we made it outside.

For the entire walk down Brookline, I was so breathless that I barely registered where we were. Shruti led me through a maze of streets that were increasingly residential. Along the way, we picked up other girls from dorms and apartments, most of them sophomores. None of them looked at me or asked who I was. But none of them questioned my being there either.

As we neared a house with thumping music bursting from the windows—the party house, I assumed—the girls passed a flask around. It smelled of the same cheap vodka on Shruti's breath. When it got to me, I balked and stared at it instead of taking it. My first mistake. The girl who held it out in her fist rolled her eyes and passed it the other way down the line. No one else had noticed.

When we finally made it to the music-thumping house, Shruti pushed open the front door, saving me from what would have been my second mistake. I had never just walked into someone's house, especially when I didn't know whose house it was—which, I realized with a thrill, was the case with this house. My parents would have died or locked me up in my room or signed me up for obedience classes like a wayward dog. As I followed the girls inside, I noticed that my face had softened into a grin.

The house was darker than I imagined it would be, which didn't make sense at first. How were you supposed to recognize people from your dorm or your classes? Certainly not by their voices either, given how loud the music was. Maybe the point was not to recognize anyone at all.

I thought it was disorienting. With the sparse lights, the music, the bodies and trash everywhere, and the hot, dense, beer-fog in the air, I felt as if I had stepped into a movie. And the strange part was, as I looked around, I found that the movie was one that almost suited me.

After a moment, I noticed that the girls were

no longer surrounding me. They had wandered off to boyfriends or the beer fridge, and I realized that I could not pick out a single one of their faces from the crowd. That was when I felt the weight of a body behind me, pressing up against my back. There were hands on my waist and hot breath against my ear, and suddenly, a hand was pushing a cup into my palm.

"You're looking sexy tonight," the boy said from behind me, tripping over the words as he said them.

My face flushed, and I could feel sweat pooling in the crevices of my neck and beneath the cups of my bra. My eyes were beginning to blur. I knew this was it, the moment I had to choose. I had already left Grace alone with Jim and Pam for the night—and thinking of Grace reminded me of Annie and Liz, and their shock if they could see me here. Now, I could sheepishly find my way back to the dorm, or I could party, really party, at this stranger's house and fall into the arms of an unknown boy. It wasn't that I'd never been around boys. But I had known my high school boyfriend forever, and we hadn't done more than kiss. I had never so much as danced with a boy I didn't even know.

The boy's hand holding out the cup became more insistent. He began to nip at my ear with too-sharp teeth.

I felt anxious, and tense, and hungry to do *something* just this once.

I took the cup, didn't look at what was inside, and gulped it down.

The party changed after that for me. The piss-colored beer, which had felt sticky on my throat, warmed me slightly, but did little else besides blur the edges of my vision. It was not unpleasant.

The boy danced behind me, swaying his hips with great urgency. I don't think it really mattered to him if I was there or not, but I danced with him, letting myself lean back against his body. Finally, eager to see what else could happen at this kind of party, I pulled away, telling him I was getting another drink.

I didn't, though, but just parked myself on the perimeter and watched. It felt like a study and an indulgence all at once. Maybe I wasn't quite a part of it, but all around me, here were people just reaching out and meeting one another, boldly feeling entitled to that right automatically. And as I stood and watched, I realized that this was the reason I was different. I had never felt entitled to any stranger's friendship. And maybe, I reasoned, this is why I had never broken out of timid, high-school Kayla. What could a more confident Kayla do?

Grace was sleeping when I got home. It was just after midnight when I walked in, not very late. She stirred and sat up when I turned on the light.

"What was that all about? Some kind of *Mean Girls* sabotage?" she asked.

I blushed and put down my purse. I was very deliberate with my movements to emphasize my sobriety—I'd only had the one drink, and had barely felt any different. "I just wanted to see what it was like," I said.

“It was charming, I’m sure,” Grace said. “Did Shruti remember how to laugh at us at that level of drunk?” I was a little surprised at her hostility, even after the treatment Shruti and her friends had given us on the Common.

“I didn’t stick with her. I mostly just wandered around.”

“Well, I’m happy for you that you tried it out. I’m going back to sleep.” I got ready for bed, too, so that I’d wake up early enough to study for Calc.

CHAPTER 4

A few weeks later, I was in the music department practice room for my Theory homework, trying to memorize the difference between what an augmented chord and a diminished chord sounded like, when Shruti opened the door and started to come in. There was a boy with her.

"Oh, sorry," she started to say when she saw that the room was occupied. "Oh, hey," she added when she saw that it was me. "Sorry, didn't realize anyone was in here. We were just going to practice."

"That's okay, I didn't lock the door," I replied.

"This is Mike. He's a grad student. We're working on a show together," Shruti said. "Mike, this is

Kayla. She lives on my hall." I was relieved, and a little surprised, that she acknowledged me and bothered to introduce us.

"That's cool. What's the show?" I asked.

"It's a scenes concert," Mike answered. "A bunch of schools around the Fenway are teaming up for it."

"Neat. And what are you a grad student in?"

"Social Work. It's a lot. I haven't had time to hang out with too many undergrads."

While he spoke, Shruti hung on his every word. I tried to keep from smirking. Mike seemed fine, but he looked a little like every other white boy I'd ever met. I supposed that the standards were lowered for straight girls when we were around so few men. Shruti, I could see, was trying to keep a tight grip on this one she had found.

"Hey, that reminds me, we're all going out to a party tomorrow night. Do you want to come?" Shruti asked.

"Who's 'we all?'" I asked immediately, mostly

because I knew she was talking to Mike. I didn't want her to forget I was there.

"Oh, uh, just some girls from Bigelow and Stanley," she said. Stanley was the dorm next door to ours. "You can come, too," she added. A low blow, to keep the upper hand and remind me I hadn't been included in the first invitation. I just smiled.

"I'd love to," I told her.

"Sure, I'll go, too," Mike said.

A smile spread over Shruti's lips, cool and calculating. "Cool. Good. Let's go see if we can find another practice room, Mike."

And they were gone.

"You're going out with them again?" Grace asked when I told her about my plans for the next night. "I thought that was a one-time thing."

Christina, who was hanging out in our room and sitting on the floor, raised an eyebrow. "You went out with Shruti?" she asked. Over the course of midterms month, she had mostly shut herself up in her room, and we hadn't seen much of her. I had never mentioned the Columbus Day weekend party.

"Yeah, just for a house party. Once. Like, a while ago."

"Oh," Christina said. Her face crumpled into a frown. I knew that her roommate had never invited her out to a party.

"And you're going again . . . why?" Grace continued.

I shrugged. "I don't know. I'm stressed out, I guess."

"Midterms are over," Grace reminded me.

"I know. But I feel like I haven't done anything all semester. You know?"

"No," Grace said, while at the same time Christina was saying, "Yeah."

Collectively, we each raised an eyebrow and exchanged quizzical looks. I don't think any of us had been particularly honest with each other, or even communicative, over the past few weeks. Or, if not dishonest, then we had not been telling whole truths.

“I bet you could come too, Christina,” I said to break the silence.

“Not my scene. Plus, I don’t think Shruti would like it.”

“There’s an improv show tomorrow night. We could do that instead,” Grace suggested.

“Yeah, let’s do that,” Christina agreed. I shook my head, determined now not to spend another weekend doing the same thing. Grace and Christina just shrugged and bent their heads over their work.

I knocked on Christina and Shruti’s door a few safe minutes after nine p.m. the next night. Christina had already left with Grace to go to the improv show. There was loud laughter coming from behind the door. It trickled away to a sputtering, and Shruti opened the door.

“Hey,” she said. Behind her in various arrays of half-dress were three other girls from her crew. “We were just getting ready.”

I nodded. I had been putting myself together for the last hour and a half to achieve a look of deliberate carelessness and ease. My outfit was simple: an oversized sweatshirt that slipped off one shoulder, cinched at the waist with a belt, and leggings. My eyes were lined with winged liner—it took three tries, but it worked—and I had blow-dried my hair out into a large, appealing puffball.

"What's the party tonight?" I asked.

"It's just a house party with some senior girls I know from tennis," one of the other girls said. I vaguely remembered that her name was Hannah. "Should be pretty small."

"Yeah, it should leave Shruti plenty of room for some *intimate* conversation," another girl laughed.

"Oh, shut up," Shruti grumbled, and threw a pillow at her. The girl shrieked.

"Watch the hair!" she cried. "You're not the only one trying tonight. There's an entire tennis team waiting for me."

"So you're really going for Mike?" I asked Shruti.

"Yeah. And Meredith is going for the entire women's tennis team, apparently."

"Now you shut up," the girl called Meredith quipped. "Just one will do."

Being in this room surrounded by banter gave me the same warm feeling I had had during the Columbus Day weekend party. For what was now the second time in college, I felt like a part of something bigger than and outside of myself. Maybe, eventually, I would even stake my own claim in the banter.

Shruti capped her mascara and turned to the girls.

"You look great," they said, or, "Perfect," before she even had to ask.

"Let's go, then," she said.

The party was not small. Either Hannah the tennis girl had been wrong, or we had different definitions of what a big party was, and I didn't care to figure out which. It was in a ratty second-floor apartment off Park Drive.

I started drinking early this time, to help me fit

in and adjust and pretend I wasn't nervous. Beer had been easy that first time around, so I felt pretty safe about handling more booze. I made my way first thing to the kitchen to take a shot of the cheap vodka that I was learning was a staple freshman beverage at parties. It burned on the way down, and I involuntarily stuck out my tongue and screwed up my eyes. I heard a laugh from behind me.

"You new to this?" It was Mike, the grad student Shruti was after. He was wearing a sweater vest and had his hair swept back in a fashionably hipster style. I could almost see the appeal as he stood there in the kitchen light.

"Yeah. I guess. Sort of," I said. Too many starts for one sentence. I poured another shot.

"Whoa there, slow it down," Mike said. I ignored him and knocked it back. "You're really not messing around, there, are you?" I wiped my mouth with the back of my hand and nodded my head toward the living room, where I had left the rest of the group.

"I think Shruti was looking for you," I told him.

"Okay. See you around, then." He wandered off to be wooed.

The rest of the party, despite the musty filth of the apartment, was bewitching. I wandered into one of the other rooms and took a moment to marvel at the presence of an equal distribution of the sexes. Maybe this party was hosted by tennis girls, but they seemed to cast a wide net far outside Simmons. I drank it in as the alcohol started to warm the liquid around my brain.

This party, like the last one, was dark. Darkness, too, appeared to be a trend at these kinds of things. I found that I liked it. It made me feel anonymous, but anonymous by choice—the kind I could break out of just by talking to someone. And talking to someone, to a stranger, was not weird, the way it would have been any other time. The people at these kinds of parties seemed completely at ease with the fact that they didn't know everyone and gave off the air that they were comfortably sure you all would meet. I needed to channel that attitude and join in.

The problem was, I still didn't know how to actually start these conversations. Going up to someone and saying, "Hi, I'm Kayla, nice to meet you" seemed more than a little hackneyed. So I would let them come to me. And, like clockwork, someone did. It was a boy I had never seen before.

"Are you on the tennis team?" he asked. I shook my head. "Good, I hate tennis," he replied. I laughed.

"Why are you here, then?"

"Why are *you* here?"

"To meet people, I guess. Not tennis players. I kind of hate it too."

"Come meet us, then. We were gonna go smoke. Wanna join?"

Shit. I was still getting used to the alcohol thing. I hadn't counted on smoking. "You mean, like, pot?" I asked. The boy laughed.

"Yeah. You smoke?"

I bit my lip. I knew my parents had given me a hard no on pot, not that I had ever asked. It wasn't a question, it was a given. Even so, they had given me piles and piles of reasons, plus piles and piles of things to say to resist peer pressure. Yet, as I stood with this stranger, all I could think was, *What would high school Kayla never do?* And the answer, glaringly, was pot.

"I'll go," I said.

The next morning, I woke up in my own bed, though I couldn't immediately recall how I had gotten there. I had a wicked headache and felt nauseated when I sat up.

Grace was at her desk with her lab manual out. "Fun night?" she asked, not looking up from the book.

"Yeah," I said, even though I couldn't remember specific details after learning how not to cough on the pot. "How was improv?"

"It turned out to be a good show," Grace replied. "We missed you."

"Sorry."

We heard two raps on the door, and I went to answer it. Hannah and Meredith, two of the girls from the party, were outside, wearing sweats. They peeked behind me when I opened the door.

"Hey! We wanted to check up on you," Hannah said, which surprised me and was a little touching.

"And also see if you went home with that guy," Meredith added, craning her neck to see around me into the room. I felt less touched. My face flushed as I tried to pretend that Grace wasn't overhearing.

"Nope. Just me. What about you guys?"

"No dice," Meredith sighed.

"Yeah, same here. And Shruti dropped Mike—he turned out to be kind of a tool," Hannah said. I wasn't exactly sure what that meant, but assumed it had something to do with the sweater vest.

"You had a hell of a night, though, girl." Meredith grinned.

"I what?"

"Poor thing doesn't remember," Hannah cooed. Meredith laughed.

"I guess cross-fading is new for you, huh? Well, you can be sure that your 'A Whole New World' duet and your sick breakdancing solo made everyone's night."

My face flushed a deeper red. As she spoke, the details started coming back to me, and I remembered a karaoke machine with a spit-damp microphone that kept bumping against my lips.

"Don't worry," Hannah assured me. "We kept an eye on you. People actually thought you were really cool. Shruti wants you to come out with us again next weekend."

"Really?"

"Yeah. She says you were the life of the whole damn party." Hannah smiled sweetly at this, but her voice came out harder than I expected.

"Wow."

"So, we'll text you about next week. Now take

these, and go take a shower. You still have your makeup on." Hannah handed me two ibuprofens and scampered down the hall with Meredith.

Grace raised her eyes and turned her head, but didn't turn all the way in her chair to face me.

"I, um, guess I'm going out next weekend," I said. She just went back to her manual.

The next weekend was a Friday-Saturday doubleheader. And it was a new beast: a frat party at Northeastern. Shruti had hooked up with a guy, or was friends with someone who had hooked up with a guy who was in a frat there, and it was convenient because Northeastern was basically down the road. The name of the frat slipped from my mind as soon as I heard it. I had only ever seen frat parties in movies, so I was excited to try it out. I ironed my hair pin-straight and pulled on the new skirt I had bought during the week, channeling Shruti for inspiration.

As I was getting ready, my classes crossed my mind for an instant when my eyes fell on a textbook resting on the floor. Up until this week, classes had been going fairly well. Calc was always a bit of a struggle, but I was caught up in everything else, even ahead in Principles of Ed. A pre-programmed part of my brain told me that it wasn't a good idea, academically, to go out twice in one weekend. But when I remembered the party from the week before and the warmth I had felt there, it was easy to silence it.

This time, the girls knocked on my door to pick me up.

"You ready?" Meredith asked.

"Almost," I said. I gave my eyelashes one last swab of mascara and picked up my keys. "Ready."

We had to go down Huntington Ave to get to the frat house. Just like before, I felt the thrill of the novelty and rebellion. Plus, on the busy street, I could feel eyes on me from everywhere. Eyes from the building-dwellers; eyes from pedestrians; eyes from the people on the trolley that thundered past us. I felt intoxicated by my own youth.

The frat house was, if possible, a step down from the dank apartments where we had been partying. The floors were sticky, and the walls seemed literally to ooze mold and beer stains and unidentifiable goo. In the basement, where the party was concentrated, I felt like I was trapped in the middle of an enormous beer gut.

To my surprise, though, the frat guys were terrifically nice. They took our coats when we came in and handed us beers right away—closed tab-top ones, too, so we didn't have to worry about them putting anything in our drinks. It was a beautiful picture of twenty-first century chivalry.

One of the boys led us to a grimy hallway where a table was set up with cups placed in precise triangles on either end. "This is beer pong," the boy said.

"We know," Shruti replied, just as I was saying, "Oh, neat!" I shut my mouth, but the boy turned to me. He was a little pimply and short, but deliciously male.

"Partner up?" he asked. I batted my eyelashes and hoped that I wasn't inadvertently stamping my cheeks with mascara.

"You're on," I said.

He called over one of his frat brothers and his skinny girlfriend, who was already hair-out-of-the-ponytail drunk. "Hey, Tony, you and Jess are on table. I'm on next with . . . "

"Kayla," I said.

"Cool. With Kayla. I'm Nick, by the way."

"Charmed," I said, and sank low into a fake curtsey. Nick laughed. Then, he filled up our cups with beer.

"This game is simple. All you need to do is get the ball in one of their cups. You sink it, they drink. They sink it in one of yours, you drink. Got it?" I nodded. "Cool. Let's go."

After a few rounds, it was clear that either I was very good at this game, or everyone else was really drunk. Jess, the girlfriend, shrieked every time I got a ball in. She really lost it when the ball slapped the surface of the beer and it splashed up out of the cup onto her top.

When all of Tony and Jess's cups were gone and Jess had burst into real tears, I turned to Nick. "I'm thirsty," I said. "I didn't get to drink any of this beer."

"Flip cup, then?" he suggested.

"Excellent."

He led me to another room—at this point, I was so confused by the maze of the basement that I wasn't sure if I had already been there—where a group of boys surrounded a table that was filled with even more cups than the beer pong table. Nick elbowed his way into a spot and pulled me along beside him.

"Make room, asswad," he shouted to the frat bro next to him. The frat bro obliged. Amid the noise and chaos of the game already in progress, Nick explained the rules to me. Finally, I drank several cups in rapid succession. I think I kissed Nick when we were done, though I couldn't be entirely sure.

The next night was another frat, this time at MIT. Surprisingly, despite a slightly higher nerd-to-chill ratio, it was much the same, right down to the sticky floors. I kissed more frat boys and didn't ask their names. With the first guy, I felt a little shallow about it. But by the time the second came along, I started to feel like I was wielding power.

After that, the weekends melted and melded into that for me. Weekdays were for catching up on sleep, and I slept through a few classes straight into the afternoon. At this point in the semester, I figured, it didn't make that much of a difference. Plus, I always made it to Principles of Ed. I was fairly confident in its being the only class I really cared about. Then, on weekends, I would meet up with the girls and pregame in Shruti's room, and then we would migrate to whatever party someone had texted Shruti about. The only things that changed were the houses and our skirts. The faces, the drinks, the words were largely the same. I grew devoutly faithful to the routine, and it loved me right back. It gave me men and pot and nicer liquor when I asked for it.

But more than that, it gave me a name. Or, rather, it gave Boston my name to do with as it pleased, which took the burden off me. It seemed that what pleased it was to spread my name throughout the Fenway, so that I was much more than a nobody or a girl in the library on a Friday night. Perhaps I wasn't anyone in particular, but I was solidly part of a group that could be recognized. Finally, I felt that I was in charge of my life and something else was in charge of my name, so that we joined forces to actually mean something.

CHAPTER 5

By the time December hit, Grace and I were barely speaking anymore. She would say, "I'm going to take a shower, please leave the door unlocked," or I would say, "I'm going to leave my desk light on for a while so I can work." And that would be it. I saw Christina only when I went to her room to pick up Shruti, and those times, she would not even look at me.

I had stopped limiting going out to the weekend. There was a club in Back Bay called The Whaling Company that was notorious for turning a blind eye to fakes on Wednesday nights, and Shruti and I started going every week, dragging along with us anyone who would come. This meant my nightly phone calls to my parents became less and less frequent. I assured my mother this would change, eager to quiet her more than anything.

"Can't you just call me to say hi? Or that you're still alive?" my mother asked me one night. "Just once a day. It's not a lot."

"*Mom*," I insisted, "I'm not just going to drop dead because I'm in college. Literally nobody calls their parents every day. So, please, just lay off. I'm stressed enough as it is with classes." This maybe wasn't entirely true, but to be fair, my new schedule was time-consuming and pretty exhausting. I didn't need the extra pressure of making up alternate stories to please my mother.

Though Boston kept getting colder and colder as December trudged along, my skirts got shorter and shorter. For maybe the first time that I could remember, I felt fresh, and alert, and a little sexy.

Meredith knocked on my door one Wednesday afternoon when I was straightening my hair to get ready to go out. This was unexpected—usually, I didn't see Shruti or her group of girls unless we were going out for the night. Grace glanced up out of habit at the knock, then went back to her book to let me answer it.

Meredith looked me up and down when I opened the door. "Are you going out tonight?" she asked.

"Yeah, WhaleCo Wednesday," I said. "Aren't you?"

"Uh, not this week. Finals."

"Finals." I tested the word out on my tongue. Finals would be held over the next two weeks. And I had forgotten about them. Or, not exactly forgotten, but just hadn't given them any thought. I wracked my brain, trying to remember anything that professors had said about finals in the last few classes. All I could remember was Dr. Lloyd's recent rant about state testing in Principles of Ed.

"You were planning on studying, right? I mean,

I don't think I can fake it," Meredith said. Her face was cut with a look of slight panic.

"Yeah, I guess I just wasn't thinking about it," I replied.

"We weren't either, really," Meredith admitted. "Until today. Shruti is in her room kind of freaking out. I thought that, um, maybe you knew a good place we could all go to study?"

It was a little bit of a jab, I thought, a reference back to the days before I started going out with them. On top of that, I was a little hurt that Meredith had this inside information about Shruti. Did they always hang out during the week when we weren't going out? But I gritted my teeth and answered, wanting to be helpful, and secretly pleased that they were including me in the study party invitation.

"Yeah," I said, "I actually have a great spot in the library." When I said this, Grace looked up again from her work, a wounded look in her eyes. She had guessed, correctly, that I was planning on bringing them to the cherished Grace-Christina-Kayla library table. She opened her mouth, debating whether to say anything. Thinking better of it, she just shook her head and returned once more to studying.

"But let's make it go down a little easier, yeah?" I added. I reached under my bed and pulled out a half-full handle of vodka. *Vodka is made out of potatoes*, a voice in my head spoke up, unsolicited. *Mashed vodka, sweet vodka, French-fried vodka. Ew.* I unscrewed the cap, poured the cheap liquor into it, and offered it to Meredith. She drank. Then, I poured some for myself and downed it. "Let's go," I said.

We collected Shruti and headed over to the academic campus to get to the library. The ground was frozen under our feet and would not thaw for months. The sky was a bright gray and looked like snow, but none had yet fallen.

I tried to make my sidelong glances toward Shruti discreet on the walk over, but it got harder the more I looked. I had never seen her like this before. Her hair was frizzy and tied back in a bun, and she was wearing a pair of thick glasses and no makeup. The real difference, though, was the look of panic on her face. Without the mask of fierce confidence I so naturally associated with her, I barely recognized her.

When we got to the library, it was busier than I remembered. Granted, I hadn't been there for at least a month, and I assumed that finals were causing the crowd. People really took this stuff seriously, didn't they?

Thankfully, our table was still free. We put down our bags and pulled out our computers, ready to try to make work happen. My brain was a little foggy from the vodka. I tried to clear it, and my focus was directed sharply to my outfit—I was still wearing the dress I had planned to wear to WhaleCo. I blushed.

Meredith saw me blushing and laughed. "You

really weren't planning on finals, were you?" she said.

"I guess not," I answered, and zeroed in on my computer screen. There was a blank Word document open on it. I hadn't written my name yet, and I wasn't even sure what class it was for. The most productive thing to do, I decided, was to look through all my syllabi and figure out everything I had to do.

I opened up all the PDFs. My PDF reader needed an update, so I did that. Then, I thought it would probably be a good idea to check all my software for updates. Just so that I would definitely be ready to do my finals.

But the whole "finals in December" thing reminded me that it was almost Christmas, and I hadn't bought any Christmas presents yet. I decided to just get a preliminary shopping list going on Amazon before I started working. That way, I wouldn't be behind, and I wouldn't disappoint my parents or Annie and Liz.

"Three pages," Meredith said suddenly.

"What?" I asked.

"I finished three pages of this paper for history. Which really isn't bad, it just needs to be five. I think I'm ready to call it a night."

I looked at the clock on my computer. Three hours had passed since we had come into the library. How had that happened? I clicked on my Word doc and found that the only thing I had written was my first name.

"Yeah, I'm good to break," Shruti said. "I got some good studying in for Psych, so I'm feeling better. This was a good idea, Kayla."

"Uh, yeah. Thanks." They were both looking at me expectantly to see what great finals feats I had accomplished. In a flash of movement, I shut my computer and leapt out of my chair to start packing up. Shruti and Meredith followed suit.

When I got back to my dorm, I opened up my computer and made a list of what I actually needed to do for finals. It was no less than:

- One Econ exam
- One Psych project
- Ten to twelve pages about an education theory
- One Calc exam
- Fifteen to twenty minutes' worth of presentation about Rachmaninoff

Doable? Maybe. Time would tell.

The next two weeks were largely a blur. I more or less took up residence in the library, claiming a quiet study carrel for myself, far away from everyone else. It was on a separate floor from the Grace-Christina-Kayla table. I imagined that Grace and Christina were still working there, but I wasn't about to check. I was too busy making sure my new social life hadn't crept up and destroyed me class-wise.

I wore sweatpants exclusively for those two

weeks. It was really quite repulsive. My hair was perpetually in the style of "finals knots," and my diet was mostly Pop Tarts and coffee. One night, I walked six blocks in a daze to Popeye's and ate an entire fried chicken family meal. It was not cute.

After late nights of typing away in the library, my Principles of Ed paper was done, and I found that it had been easier than I expected to write about the history of elementary education theory. The Psych project got done, too, and I wrapped it all into a neat chart that analyzed children's psychology experiments. That was a risk. Leslie Leopold, renowned scholar, would either love it or rip it to shreds.

All that was left, then, were the exams—both math-based, both terrifying—and the presentation. My study carrel and I got good and cozy with one another while I worked through problem sets late into the night while blasting Rachmaninoff on my headphones. The only thing that kept me calm was the little water bottle, inconspicuously filled with vodka, that I carried back and forth to the library with me. I didn't need it, and I knew I wasn't going out, but it was comforting to dull my mind just enough to all the realities outside my finals, and to remind myself I was not the same girl I had been at the beginning of the fall.

The Econ exam and Rachmaninoff presentation were scheduled for the same day, which really wasn't fair. The finals gods were almost certainly working against me, and had been since the whole damn exam period started. The night before, I felt all right about the Econ, but had only Rachmaninoff melodies in my head and no concrete presentation. I decided to pull an all-nighter to work on the presentation rather than chance sleeping through the exam.

This was a risky plan, since Calc would be the following day, and who knew what zombie-like state of non-sleep I would be in by then. Still, given the choices, it seemed like the best option. I got to work in the library (blessedly open twenty-four hours a day during finals period, which was both a godsend and a little terrifying) and hunkered down for the night, and I actually put together a halfway-decent slideshow, all slideshows considered.

By the time the sun was coming up—and there is really nothing as picturesque as watching the sunrise through tinted library windows to the sound of quietly sobbing undergrads—I felt at peace, and also like I wanted to pour coffee directly into my eyes. All my senses felt about a half second behind schedule. But I was functional.

At eight a.m., I ventured over to the café and treated myself to a latté and a croissant. Feeling fueled-up and ready, I headed to the Econ exam early.

Plowing through the exam was cruel, but doable. Though alert from the caffeine, I felt a tiredness deep in my bones. At this point, the tiredness didn't stop me from doing the work; it only made everyday tasks, like holding a pencil, feel a little strange and foreign. I read the questions slowly and carefully, and answered every one.

By the time I got to the music department for my presentation, I was tired enough to feel like I was walking in a dream. I mumbled through my presentation and grinned stupidly at inexplicable moments, but I made it through. I even let my eyelids droop as I watched my classmates present.

By the time evening fell, I was exhausted. It was a level of exhaustion that I had never experienced firsthand, but imagined it was the kind they depicted in movies when women did things like give birth on the Oregon Trail. I was in my room, staring at the wall and thinking about going to bed, when my phone buzzed.

SHRUTI (6:14pm): FINALS DONE. coming out tonight?

Of course Shruti would be done when I was still struggling along and had my hardest final to go. I spent a good split second cursing the injustice that was college.

KAYLA (6:15pm): four down but still one to go. calc tomorrow. X_X

SHRUTI (6:16pm): take a break!! you deserve it, plus you'll do better if you're relaxed.

I thought about it. She was right, I kind of *did* deserve it. The past two weeks had been a sort of lonely hell. I hadn't gone out once, and all I'd had to drink was my water-bottle vodka. And at this point, a few more hours wouldn't make much of a difference for Calc. I really would feel better if I relaxed for a few hours and then got some sleep.

KAYLA (6:18pm): okay. when & where?

SHRUTI (6:19pm): great. soccer house, 8pm.

I set my phone alarm for seven-thirty, then fell into a deep sleep until it was time to get ready to go.

Soccer House was not actually for Simmons soccer, but was a house where a bunch of guys from some other school's soccer team all lived. I could never remember which school it was. When Shruti and I got there, all of our usual crowd in tow, it appeared that everyone from the colleges of the Fenway who had finished their finals was there. Beer flowed freely from a keg in the kitchen, and every variety of drinking game was going on in one room or another. I felt like I was in a fairytale caricature of my own semester.

Most of the girls stuck around in the kitchen while some of the soccer players tried to figure out what a keg stand was, and how to do one—they really didn't know. Shruti and I made our way to a room where they were playing a game called Top Shelf. We had never heard of it.

"You just kind of follow along," one of the soccer players told us, "and try to figure out the rules as you go. We'll tell you when to drink." Shruti giggled and sat on his lap. I took a seat across the table.

My sleep-deprived mind was in no state for this game. As we passed cups and dice back and forth, I couldn't comprehend what anyone was saying, never mind figuring out the rules of this made-up game. I just kept passing and passing, while they shouted, "DRINK!," at me over and over. I obeyed.

And soon, it caught up with me. The gum I'd had for dinner. My sleepless night. All the stress of finals. The room melted into a swirl of lights and colors around me, gradually at first, and then in a hurry. I could hear the bass line of the music and too-loud laughter. The table began to spin and I felt a boy's arm around me, and at one point, someone stuffed a mozzarella stick in my mouth. Then, everything was dark.

When I opened my eyes, I was in a sterile white room that I definitely did not recognize and that definitely did not belong to one of the soccer boys. There was an IV in my arm, and my stomach felt like a shipwreck. My head was pounding, and I couldn't lift it.

Even in my clouded state of mind, I could put the pieces together. Last night had been a for-real blackout. So real that it landed me in the hospital. I felt the blood drain from my face as I came to the realization, and my previously immobile head jerked upward on a reflex. My head could move, and all my limbs appeared to be where they belonged—I was still alive.

After a few minutes, a nurse walked in. She had a thick Boston accent. "Good, hon, you're awake," she said. Her face was stern. "You know, I keep seeing this with college kids. You need to watch the drinking. You're lucky you had a friend to bring you in."

I was surprised and a little bit touched that Shruti had brought me here instead of leaving me to drown in my own vomit. At least, I assumed it was Shruti. I remembered her being with me during the drinking game before my memory cut out. "It was an accident," I said weakly.

“Not many people get their stomachs pumped for fun, kid. Now, we’ll just make sure you’re patched up and get you out of here.”

That was when it hit me. *Out of here.* What time was it? I gulped and peeked out the window. The skyline betrayed that it was definitively mid-morning. Roughly translated, that meant mid-Calc exam. And I was in a bed in the emergency room, just back from flirting with death.

The nurse, who must have been trained for this sort of thing, noticed when my breathing sped up and I started to sweat.

“I know, kid,” she said. “It’s finals. But don’t worry. Your school will get documentation about this. You’ll have your excuse.” She gave me a sweet-ish smile, the sort of smile that told me she was a matriarch who was sick of kids screwing around. And here I was, prime offender.

I thought about Shruti and how she wasn’t here now. Presumably, she was safely back at Simmons, laughing at her incompetent friend, and maybe even spicing up the story so it would be juicier for the other girls. So I would fail Calc, and Simmons would know all about my passing-out, stomach-pumping drinking, and she had abandoned me. That *bitch*.

A few days later, I packed up my room to go home for break. The whole time, Grace sat silently at her desk and refused to even look at me. Everything felt a little surreal. I was in a state of non-belief about what had happened after the "done-with-finals" party, and I didn't know what would happen next. I had never failed a class before. Nor had I almost *died* before. By then, my body felt mostly back to normal, if a little queasy. But when I let my mind delve into the details of that night, I was terrified by the vulnerability of my body.

When I was ready to go, I stopped by the campus mail center. There was an official-looking envelope in my box with a stamp from the Dean of the College. I tore it open.

Dear Kayla Howard,

This letter is to inform you that you will be required to attend a hearing with Dean Storey before the start of the spring semester due to your reported misconduct. Please be advised that your status as an undergraduate student at Simmons College will be determined at this hearing. Simmons takes reports of misconduct seriously, as we strive to make our campus a safe academic environment for all students.

Your hearing is scheduled for January 15, 2016 at 8:30am in Dean Storey's office. Before that time, we encourage you to make every effort to complete your assignments for MATH0200: Fundamentals of Calculus, for which you have received a grade of Incomplete.

Sincerely,
The Dean of the College

A dean's hearing. A dean's hearing that would determine whether or not I could even come back to school. I never, ever thought that I would be one of those kids.

So what was I now?

CHAPTER 6

I didn't see much of anyone for the first few days of winter break. There were the required family gatherings for Christmas, and I mimed my way through them, but I kept to myself when I could, and didn't say much of anything. My parents, to my surprise and delight, left me alone at first and did not question my near-silence. Maybe it was just the rush and stress of the holidays, or maybe they could feel the negative energy exuding out of me. I didn't believe in things like positive and negative energy, but I felt so grim, so repulsive in those early days of break, that I seemed to be constantly surrounded by a cloud of my own revilement.

This grace period ended on New Year's. My parents had the same plans they had every year—plans that they absolutely would not break—to eat fancy cheeses with their book club friends and watch celebrities lip sync as a ball inched down on television. I, on the other hand, was unsure what a home-for-a-few-weeks college kid was supposed to do on New Year's Eve. Did everyone see people from high school? Did they still have friends from high school? Were there bars that would let us in, and if there were, would I want to risk it? I hadn't had a drink in almost two weeks, and I was worried I wouldn't know how to socialize anymore without alcohol.

My parents finally broke their nonchalance and asked me what my New Year's plans were. I considered my answer carefully. I could stock up on brownie points before they knew anything about the dean's hearing—I could say I was going to scrub the house clean and bake cookies for the homeless. But that might seem suspicious. I could say what was likely, which is that I would lie on my bed and watch Netflix. Instead, I went with my default safe answer.

"Um, I guess I'll see what Liz and Annie are up to," I said. I hadn't heard from them in months. To be fair, I hadn't texted them either. Though I often thought of them, it was surprisingly difficult to stay in touch when we weren't in the same place, even though they had been my best friends when we were all in New Jersey.

"Good," my dad answered. "I haven't heard about them lately. What are they up to?"

Oh gosh. "I'll probably have a better answer for you when I meet up with them." *Real smooth about it.* My dad just chuckled.

So, the afternoon of New Year's Eve, I sent out a group text. I was a little surprised to see, when I typed in their names, that the last text in the thread was from the early days of orientation, and I had sent it: miss you guys!! xoxo, followed by the emoji that blows a kiss. I didn't remember writing it.

Time to revive it, I thought. I wrote, hey! home for break. you guys have plans for tonight? I sat back and waited for a response, which was strangely nerve-wracking. I had never before been stressed out when texting my two best friends. But what if they didn't count as my best friends anymore if the fall semester had been a total bust for our friendship? Was it normal to totally ditch your friends during your first semester of college, or was that the exact sort of thing a terrible friend would do?

I sat tense in my room as I waited for them to respond. My phone buzzed five minutes later.

ANNIE (2:56pm): hey! Dan and I were just gonna stay in. did you have plans?

LIZ (2:58pm): stay in… and do what, play bridge? live a little.

Oh gosh, witty banter. Had they stayed completely normal friends this whole time, and I was the only one who had jumped ship?

KAYLA (2:59pm): no plans for me. :(let's meet up?

LIZ (3:03pm): sounds good. when/where?

ANNIE (3:04pm): we could do Kristen's, maybe around 10.

KAYLA (3:05pm): cool! see you guys then.

Kristen's, that was a trip. I hadn't been to Kristen's since maybe July. It was the pub where kids used to hang out in high school, mostly to eat burgers after football games. Townies hung out there, too, since the bar opened at three in the afternoon.

I bounded into the kitchen with more energy than I'd had since break began. My mom was pulling meat off a chicken—I thought, somehow, that she was plucking its feathers at first—while my dad read the paper. He still read the physical copy.

"I'm going out with Annie and Liz tonight," I announced.

"Oh, good," my dad said.

"Have fun. Be home by twelve," my mom added, not looking up from the chicken.

I gaped at her. "You know it's New Year's, right? Like, that was a reflex. Right?"

She turned to face me, wrist-deep in the chicken. "All the crazies will be out tonight, Kayla," she said.

"You'll be out tonight," I pointed out.

"But all the crazies, too. It's dangerous."

"You can't seriously want me to skip midnight on New Year's."

"I just don't want you coming home at all hours of the night and getting hit by a drunk driver."

"Mom. We're just going to Kristen's. I promise you it will be alright."

She sighed. "Just be careful, please."

I drove my mother's car to Kristen's just before ten. The parking lot was nearly full. I spotted Liz's car, sporting a new Penn bumper sticker, and Annie's car a few spots down. This was good. If they were already here, I wouldn't have to wait all by myself.

Inside, the restaurant was dark and smelled like stale cigarettes. People were crowded around the bar in an equitable meeting of the old and young. I spotted Annie and Liz at a low table near the door, sipping on glasses of water.

"Hey!" I called to them. They rose, and I hugged them each in turn. "It's really good to see you guys," I said, meaning it.

"Oh man, I missed you both," Liz said. "I mean, Penn is great, but it's no Jersey."

"Rutgers is pretty Jersey," Annie admitted, "but Dan's friends are not you guys. Or ladies."

"Well, Simmons is *just* ladies," I retorted. "As I may have mentioned. It's a lot."

"Wait, so you actually never see guys now?" Liz asked.

"Not never. There are some grad students who are guys. Plus . . . " I considered telling them about the parties, about the Emmanuel guys and the BU guys and the Harvard guys. But that would involve telling them about the drinking and all the things I had never done just months before. It was too risky. I didn't even know if we were still friends. How had I not thought of this before? "Plus," I continued, "it's a city, so guys are really everywhere."

"I'm definitely finding that, too," Liz agreed. "But I don't have time for dating, really. School and everything takes a hell of a lot of time."

"What are you guys doing, though? I mean, what's your thing in college? I feel like we haven't actually talked in months," Annie said.

"I joined rugby!" Liz said. "I never thought I'd be a sports person, but it's actually great. And there's the paper, of course. Journalism is kind of kicking my ass." Liz was a journalism major, which she had been planning on since middle school.

"I hear that," Annie agreed. "I feel like I spend my entire life on nursing stuff. Then, I just come home to Dan and crash."

Liz sighed and shook her head. "Shit, I thought college was supposed to be fun. It seems like we're just old. Kayla, are you having that, too?"

"I, um. I had this really interesting Education

Studies class. The professor was kind of intense, but in a cool way, you know?"

"Are you majoring in Education Studies, then?" Annie asked innocently.

"Well, I haven't exactly decided yet."

"That's okay, you still have, like, a year to figure it out," Liz reassured me. "So what other stuff have you been focusing on instead?"

Things I could not say included parties, frats, beer, pot brownies, and kissing strangers. Annie and Liz had given me no indication they'd encountered any of these things—had they changed from high school at all? "Just adjusting, I guess," I decided on. I sipped from the unclaimed glass of water. Somehow, it was as if I hardly knew them anymore. I couldn't tell them a thing about my new, real life.

Thankfully, Dan showed up at the table then. I hadn't been sure if he would join us, but I was very happy to see him at that moment, especially since he was carrying a plate of nachos. He put them in the center of the table before bending down to kiss the top of Annie's head.

"*Yesss,*" Liz breathed. We all dug in and devoured the plate. Nobody said a single word. Then, too soon, the plate was empty.

There were a lot of things I wanted to say to them and ask them. *What do you actually, for real, do on the daily? Who are your friends? Am I replaced? Have I replaced you?* I couldn't say any of them. I couldn't remember what was appropriate anymore, or what was the common ground on which we met.

Silently, we looked at one another.

Then, a girl who had been in our high school class, Joanna, drifted past the table. "Annie! Hey!" she called. She had an electric-blue drink in her hand that I was pretty sure was alcoholic, even though I knew she was eighteen or nineteen like the rest of us. Even after my fall semester, I didn't know how to pull that off in New Jersey.

"Oh, hi," Annie said. "You guys remember Joanna, right?" We nodded.

"Annie and I had some classes together at Rutgers," Joanna said. "And . . . " she gave Dan a quizzical look.

"Dan," he said.

"Right. Dan." She giggled. "Well, see you guys around. Happy New Year's!"

We followed the driveway rule and waited until she was out of earshot. "She's kind of a vapid idiot," Annie said, which was a very un-Annie-like thing to say.

"And her dress is short as hell," Liz added. "I feel like I had sex with her just by looking at her."

"Was she like that in high school?" Dan asked.

"I need to pee," I announced, and made a straight shot for the bathroom.

For once, I was happy about what I had learned during the fall semester—I knew enough to squat over the toilet on New Year's. I felt vaguely nauseous, but decided to leave before I gave serious thought to throwing up.

Joanna was standing over the sink touching up

her makeup when I came out of the stall. I washed my hands and considered her out of the corner of my eye.

"So, um, how'd you get that drink?" I asked her.

She smiled and turned to me. "The old high school stuff not really your scene anymore?"

"Not really," I admitted.

"Me either. I've decided to branch out a little."

"I want to, too, but I can't really. Not here."

"I know what you mean. I didn't come out until I got to college. But I guess it was easier for you, right, going to Simmons?"

"Um. What was easier?"

"Coming out," she said.

"You think I'm a lesbian?"

"Well, you're at an all-girls school, so—"

"I can't believe you're seriously saying that. Is that actually still a thing?"

Joanna looked at me, thin-lipped and wide-eyed, unable to think of anything to say.

"I'm not a lesbian. You can't make a freaking

assumption like that. Simmons is just where I ended up, I can't help it."

I ripped a paper towel from the dispenser and scrubbed my hands dry. Then I thrust the door open and slammed it on my way out.

When I got back to the table, still fuming, we listened to Liz give us rugby play-by-plays. I could barely concentrate on what she said, as I was so frustrated with where Simmons had left me. Liz talked until the silent minute before midnight. Then, the lights all went down in Kristen's, and we watched the New Year's ball drop on a huge TV screen. Just like my parents were doing.

"So what did you do last night?" my mother asked the next morning.

"I told you, I went to Kristen's," I said.

"Who'd you go with?"

"Did you forget? Annie and Liz. Who else would I even go with?"

"You don't need to snap at me, Kayla."

I hadn't meant to. My head hurt inexplicably, and I felt more tired than I had all semester, as if everything had caught up with me at once. The dawn of the New Year told me starkly that time had really passed, and there was a real dean's hearing waiting for me in just weeks. My entire future was in a precarious balance. In the effort to hide it from my parents, all I could do was lash out.

It got worse as the week went on. I avoided my parents outside of dinnertime, which we invariably spent together. They vaguely scowled at me as they said less and less each night.

"Kayla," my dad said one night, "is there something wrong? You've been awfully quiet."

"I'm not quiet. You're quiet," I shot back. *Good one, Kayla.*

"He's right, hon," my mother added. "Did

something happen at school? Did you not like it? You've barely told us a thing about it."

"Nothing happened. It's just school. It's stressful."

"You said you'd tell us if you needed something. You didn't tell us anything."

"I'm fine. Sorry. I guess I just need some time alone."

Both my parents frowned at me, and I could see in their eyes that they didn't believe me. For a split second, I thought about spilling everything and telling them about the dean's hearing. Surely, they would fix it. They would know what to do, and they would help me figure out what the hell I was doing in college. But that was impossible.

The last few days of break were a nearly endless nightmare. I spent most of my time in my room watching Netflix and TED talks. It was a strange and pathetic combination that I would have laughed at, had anyone else done it.

Mostly, I tried to avoid my parents so that I wouldn't have to answer any more questions about school. When they asked about my grades, I told them I hadn't gotten them back yet. When dinner conversations turned irrevocably to "things I had learned in college," I talked extensively about the library and what a good place it was to study.

I could see the looks of concern in my parents' eyes. I wasn't sure if it was concern for the hapless geek I was portraying, or because they knew it was a big, fat lie. But I let them limit the worrying to those things. I could not, under any circumstances, tell them about the dean's hearing. It would make them furious, or worse, disappointed.

CHAPTER 7

It was not easy to think of a reasonable excuse to convince my parents to let me go back to Simmons early for my hearing. I decided to tell them there was a freshman retreat before classes started that Simmons had planned at the last minute. They not only bought it, but thought that a retreat would be a great idea and might help me get my attitude back in order. The number of times I heard the phrases "attitude adjustment" and "she needs to get off her high horse" from them was a little extraordinary. I hadn't seen the likes of it since I was about thirteen.

Nevertheless, I was on the train back to Boston

a day before my hearing with the dean. We pulled up into South Station early in the afternoon. Despite everything, or maybe because of it, South Station felt like home. This was strange, since the part of the city with South Station was perhaps the least homelike part of Boston. But there was a bright sign in the station that read *Boston Welcomes You*, and I really believed this ambiguous Boston-person.

I got onto the Red Line to make the familiar transfer at Park, where already the platform was bustling with life I hadn't seen for weeks in New Jersey. The harmonica-and-guitar guy was there, and the teenage virtuoso girl who played the violin, and the MBTA employees cracking jokes about the tourists and each other.

All the way to Simmons on the Green Line, I felt warm and full under my scarf and sweaters with the feeling of being back. Creeping beneath the surface, though, was the knowledge that in less than twenty-four hours, it might all be gone. If I hadn't:

1. Tried to impress Shruti
2. Ditched Grace and Christina
3. Started going to every party I heard about
4. Pretended to understand drinking
5. Gotten sloppy with said drinking
6. Gone to college with an impressively empty idea of what I was

And the list went on . . . If I hadn't done all these things, then maybe my entire future wouldn't be hanging on an early-morning, pre-semester hearing that was, by my estimation, more or less impossible to prepare for.

When I got back to my room, it was eerily silent. This made sense, since no one was back yet, but that didn't make it feel any less like a horror movie. I turned on the lights and opened the closet doors and all our dresser drawers, and I felt a little better.

Unpacking made me feel better, too. I unpacked everything and emptied all my bags as though there were no question about whether I would be staying. My closet looked better in color.

Once my things were unpacked, I pulled out my computer and looked at the to-do list that had remained untouched since the end of the semester. Most of the items were room-related, and I sheepishly scanned the room to see that Grace had done them all. *Take out the trash and recycling. Close the storm windows. Turn off the radiator. Unplug electronics.* I was one hell of a roommate.

Everything else on the list was Calc: *Problem sets, weeks 7 through 13. Final exam. FINAL EXAM.* Most of that could have—and probably should have—been done over break. But the whole time, I hadn't been able to bring myself to do math problems for a school that might not even let me back in. Those chapters of my book remained virginal and clean.

I slammed the computer shut and hoped a second later that the force hadn't shattered the screen. I opened it back up to double check—it hadn't. There was nothing else to do but to pick out an outfit for tomorrow that said, "cute, but not slutty, and definitely worthy of staying in your school." The options were surprisingly many—all from the beginning of the fall semester.

When that was done, I took a long, hot shower, ate a sleeve of crackers for dinner, and crawled into my bed to watch reruns of *The Office* until I fell asleep.

In the morning, I initially mistook my alarm for a funeral knell, and I wasn't even kidding. My stomach was turning violent flips as I stretched my tights over my legs and pulled my hair back into a no-nonsense bun. I picked up my pocketbook and tried to figure out what to bring with me. What was even proper at this sort of thing? A notebook? Breath mints? My Calculus book?

I decided on the letter they had sent me with the date of the hearing.

I left fifteen minutes early, even though it was only about a five-minute walk to campus. That turned out to be a good choice, since I had to walk slowly on the newly icy and slippery sidewalks. Even still, I got to the main campus building a few minutes early.

Unlike the dorms, the offices in the main campus building were as busy as ever. I had not ever really thought about the people who worked in the college offices, but it made sense that they didn't get a month off just because we weren't in classes. Things had to get done, and I supposed the semester didn't just start of its own accord.

I took some deep breaths as I stood outside the dean's office, then knocked on the door. "Come in," a voice called.

I walked into what was definitely an office. I guess I was expecting some kind of courtroom with the dean in the judge's seat and me on the witness stand. But in the room were just a desk covered with papers, and a round table where three people were seated: Dean Storey; a woman I did not recognize; and Dr. Lloyd, my professor from Principles of Ed.

"Miss Howard?" Dean Storey asked when I stepped inside.

"You can call me Kayla," I said automatically. Dean Storey raised an eyebrow. She knew what she could call me.

"Miss Howard. Have a seat," she went on. I took the empty chair at the table. "Now, Miss Howard, as I'm sure you are aware, you are here today because of an incident toward the end of the fall semester involving alcohol."

I was, in fact, aware. "Yes, ma'am."

"This incident involved not just underage drinking, but excessive underage drinking, to the point that you were transported off-campus for medical treatment. Is that correct?"

"Yes, ma'am."

"I see. And you are aware that this behavior is strictly against the student code of conduct, I assume?"

Of course I was aware. I tried to read her face, or at least look for some clues in it, but it was a mask. "Yes, I am aware," I said.

"In speaking with your professors, Miss Howard, it seems that your academic performance, which was initially quite good, dropped off at a certain point during the semester. I assume that this was the result of your habits with alcohol. As we place a high value on both student safety and academic success, not to mention, of course, the law, we do not tolerate this kind of behavior at Simmons. Your conduct is grounds for expulsion."

Oh gosh, I thought, *here it comes. How could this happen so fast? And why would they call me back for a hearing just to tell me they had already made a decision?*

"Now," the dean continued, "I would like for you to explain to us what is going on here."

Explain what was going on? Like, defend myself? Well, here it was, the exact kind of question I could have prepared for, and didn't.

"I . . . " My voice shook, and my hands, too. "I

don't know, to be honest. This is not who I am. I've never been a partier or anything, and it just sort of happened." My eyelids started to quake, and I realized in sudden horror that I was on the brink of tears. No matter what happened, I could *not* cry in front of this table full of adults.

"Why is it that you want to stay at Simmons, Miss Howard? Why should we give you another chance?" Dean Storey went on. I cleared my throat.

"I'd like to prove myself, ma'am. I'd like to show you all, and show myself, that I belong here." *I want to figure out why I want it*, I didn't say.

The dean's face softened. "Kayla," she said, "no one here wants to see you fail. These rules, and this hearing, for that matter, are in place for your benefit, not Simmons's. I have been speaking to your professor here," and here she gestured toward Dr. Lloyd, "and she assures me that at your best, you were a force to be reckoned with in class. She has tirelessly lobbied on your behalf."

I was shocked. Who knew that tough,

no-nonsense Dr. Lloyd would swoop in to save my college career? Who knew I had made that sort of impression? Sure, education theory had come easily to me, but I had no idea that my professor had actually cared. Dr. Lloyd flashed a small smile at me, and I couldn't help but smile back.

"We want to see you succeed," the dean said. "That's why you were admitted to Simmons in the first place. Still, we take your behavior from last semester extremely seriously. I have decided that you will be conditionally readmitted this term. Pending appropriate conduct, the completion of your incomplete Calculus class from last semester, and good academic standing for this semester, you will be allowed to continue pursuing your degree at Simmons without further sanction."

I let out a long, cool breath that got stuck in my throat, which then made me choke on a little bit of saliva, but I was ecstatic. I could *stay*. After everything I had messed up, and an entire break stressing about it, I was somehow, miraculously, going to stay.

"Oh, thank you, Dean Storey," I breathed. "Really, thank you!"

She went on as if I hadn't spoken. "You will also be assigned a tutor for the spring semester to help you get back to the standard of academic excellence we expect of the young women in our program. This will be a requirement for the length of the semester. Mrs. Mello here will take you to her office and give you your tutoring schedule." The woman I did not know smiled and nodded her head.

"Kayla," the dean said, softening once more, "I do wish you luck with this semester. And I expect *not* to have to see you again until we check in at the end of the spring. We will be in touch then."

This, apparently, was a cue to leave, because everyone stood up when she said it. I followed suit. Mrs. Mello left the office first, but Dr. Lloyd hung back a moment so that we walked through the door together.

"You didn't have to do that," I said. "But thanks. Really. I don't know how to thank you enough."

"We have to hold on to the ones who are going somewhere, Kayla," Dr. Lloyd replied. She smiled once more, and then started back toward her office with a flourish.

I followed Mrs. Mello down the hall in a daze, my chest feeling half-made of warm water. I couldn't stop smiling, and I was already planning my trip to the bookstore for all the course books I had been too afraid to buy ahead of time.

Grace got back to campus the next day. I heard her key in the door when I was sitting at my desk and writing out my classroom numbers for the classes that I would, gloriously, be able to take: Biology, The British Novel, Education Theory and Practice, Business Management, and French.

Grace struggled with the key for a minute, then finally popped the door open. I lifted my head when she came in.

"Hi," I said.

"Hi."

"Did you have a good break?"

"Yeah. You?"

"Yeah."

We looked at each other silently, unmoving. After what felt like a century of this, I broke the silence.

"Look, Grace, I'm really sorry. I don't want to be a jerk this semester."

Grace didn't say anything. Then, behind her in the doorframe appeared a tall, ridiculously handsome guy who had to be at least a junior and didn't attend Simmons.

"Kayla," Grace said, "this is Gao. We met at a track party at the end of last semester. He's from Harvard."

"Oh. Hi. I'm Kayla." This was startling for two reasons: First, Grace had been going to parties (undoubtedly classier than the kind I went to, but still parties), and I hadn't known, and I would never not be a terrible friend. And second, if she had come literally armed with her new boyfriend, what chance did I have in the first place to fix things?

Gao gave me a brusque nod, then averted his eyes and followed her inside. She couldn't have told him anything good about me. The two of them unpacked Grace's things and listened to Hozier, easy with each other in a way that felt both shocking and natural. I put on my headphones, finished up my class list, and got to work on my incomplete. Classes were one day away.

My first tutoring session was a week after classes began, apparently to give both the tutor and me time to settle into our schedules. I had made it the whole week without going out—and I didn't leave my room unless it was strictly necessary—so I didn't see Shruti and company either. I hadn't heard from Shruti all break, not even to check on me after I'd had my stomach pumped. She never even mentioned the incident. It was strange, and it made me wonder all the more what had really happened that night.

On the other hand, even though I intended to avoid them, I was hurt by the fact that none of my fall "friends" reached out to me. I wracked my brain—and my texts—to try to figure it out. Had I always been the one to initiate plans, and now they had no intention to see me? Or had they heard about what happened and decided to shut me out?

The one thing I had control over was my classes, so I was determined to put my all into the tutoring sessions. The night of my first session, I showed up at the tutoring center right on time. The center was dangerously close to Dean Storey's office, which was either a coincidence or a highly effective scare tactic. I was surprised to find that even now, this early in the semester, the center was busy. I gave my name to the bored-looking student worker at the desk.

"Have a seat," the student said. "Your tutor will be out in a minute." Just like a doctor's office.

I sat in one of the plush chairs and ran my fingers along the edges of my Calculus notebook. The week-seven problem set was halfway done, which was maybe not ideal, but was definitely something. I also had my copy of *Brideshead Revisited* with me in the hopes that maybe I could get an early start on my English paper.

Before long, a door that led to the study cubicles opened, and a familiar-looking man stepped out.

"Kayla!" His eyes lit up when he saw me.

I took a moment to place him, and then I remembered. "Mike! Hey, good to see you." It was the grad student Shruti had been trying to hook up with months before in the fall. His smile was warm, and he was more handsome than I had remembered. Then, it clicked: *Mike.* That was my tutor's name. When Mrs. Mello had written down my tutoring information, I had been so wrapped up in my happiness over the hearing that I hadn't noticed that I knew who the tutor was, or even that it was a boy. Now, I wasn't sure whether to be friendly or mortified, but I was leaning heavily toward mortified.

Mike, however, had decided fiercely on friendly, and I was afraid for a second that he would try to hug me. He checked himself, though, and just ushered me back into one of the cubicles.

"This is great," Mike said. "I never get to work with people I know. It's easier, don't you think? Lets your guard down." I did not think so, actually. On the contrary, I thought there was little worse than being the dumb girl assigned to this apparently brilliant grad student. But none of this seemed to cross Mike's mind; or, if it did, he was determined not to let it show. "So, what are we working on?" he asked.

I opened my notebook to the week-seven problem set. "Integrals, mostly," I replied. There were some ugly graphs drawn on the page. I was hoping he would help me draw even more.

"Cool," he said. "What else? What are your other classes?" I listed them off. "You're taking six, then? That's a lot," he told me.

"Well, no, not six . . . " What was I supposed to say? Had the tutoring center not told him that he was tutoring a girl who was basically on probation? Either way, there was no way I was about to spill my story about last semester to this guy I barely knew. "It's a long story," I finally said.

To my relief, he laughed. "That's okay," he said. Then, as if reading the nerves on my face, he continued, "You know, we get a lot of the top students in here. I'm not supposed to talk about the people who come in, but it's true. Some people think they're insecure, but really, they just want to go at this college thing as hard as they can."

I gave him a weak smile for the effort, genuinely grateful at his attempt to put me at ease. "Then, everyone else is afraid of us," he went on, smiling. "But who could be afraid of this face?" Then, he made his eyes go big and dropped his lip in a perfect puppy-dog face. I laughed. For that evening, anyway, I felt like maybe this was all really doable.

CHAPTER 8

I fell quickly into a routine with my new set of classes. I was surprised at how easy it was. Part of it, I think, was that they started first thing in the morning and were scheduled one right after the other, so I had no choice but to follow their regimented order. Mondays, Wednesdays, and Fridays were Bio, then French, then Education Theory. Tuesdays and Thursdays were Business Management, then English, then Bio lab. On those days, I went to the tutoring center to meet with Mike after dinner.

I was done with class every day by one p.m., which gave me time to have lunch in the cafeteria and then do my homework and reading in the library. I took new ownership of my finals study carrel and made a secret vow to the desk that I wouldn't let it down or bring any more vodka water bottles. The schedule was so effective that I was usually done with my work by nightfall. I even had time to read for fun.

The only problem was that it was lonely. Grace was always either out with Gao or silently studying in our room. She still got up in the morning for early track practice, but we didn't go back to our morning banter from the beginning of the fall. Sometimes, she stayed overnight at Harvard, and so I didn't even see her until the next evening.

Christina, meanwhile, had persisted in orchestra and won herself a few friends. I imagined her fighting off uppity orchestra members with just her flute, waving it back and forth in their faces and maybe taking out an eye or two. She had even gotten a girlfriend, a serious viola player who was well-connected in the orchestra scene.

Everyone seemed to be settled and to have something going for them. And, as it tends to go, when people have things going well for them, they are also remarkably talented at making and keeping groups of friends. Somehow, in messing that up the first time around, I seemed to have forfeited my social life.

Grace and Christina were, understandably, rather uninterested in rekindling our trio. As for Shruti and her posse, I avoided them like the plague. Early in the semester, I had run into one of them and she asked me to go out, still with no mention of the terrible night of the blackout. When I floundered, she didn't press me on it, but none of them asked me again. When I stopped getting messages in our group text, I assumed that they had started a new one without me.

I couldn't tell if I missed them or if I just missed having people. What had started out as anger at Shruti for presumably getting me into trouble soon turned into some pretty extreme loneliness. When you are a freshman, loneliness wins out fast.

The worst part was that I couldn't even go back to Annie and Liz, my best friends from home, the girls I was always supposed to have in my life. I had ruined that over break, seeing them only at New Year's and keeping practically everything from them—not that they had tried very hard to learn about my life. There was no way I could come crawling back now. This was a deep hole, and I had dug it myself.

To my surprise, I soon found a friend in Mike. It was mostly out of necessity, but I started actually enjoying our tutoring sessions. I found myself looking forward to Tuesday and Thursday evenings, just to have someone to breathe the same air with. Plus, with no one and nothing to lose, I could talk to him about anything. Just like he had predicted, I let my guard down, but not just academically. In my desperation, I dropped all defenses and latched onto his friendship.

"What ever happened between you and Shruti?" I asked him one night.

Mike laughed. "Shruti is very much a soprano," he said.

"What does that mean?"

"Basically, that she would go well with a tenor, but I'm a baritone. She's a good singer, and I was glad to work on the concert with her last fall, but she was looking for something she wasn't going to get."

"You talk about it like you're a real hot commodity," I said.

"I call 'em as I see 'em. Now, did you finish the week-seven problem set?"

Over the course of the tutoring, I had ended up telling him that I hadn't finished Calc last semester. He didn't know all the details, but he knew that I had an incomplete and seven weeks' worth of problem sets to do. Mike wasn't particularly good at Calc himself, but he was excellent at keeping me on track.

And on track was definitely the theme of the semester so far. I had never been so caught up, or even ahead, in my classes, not even in high school. When I was putting this much time into school, I barely needed a tutor, and so Mike and I ended up spending a lot of our sessions just talking. Before long, I stopped noticing the power differential and even the age difference between us. He told me about social work and his field assignment at a nursing home, and I mostly just listened. I spent hours wishing I had my own passion, my own *thing* to talk about on Tuesday and Thursday nights. I had yet to find that thing.

And then, my field study happened. It was the "practice" part of Education Theory and Practice. I had begun almost looking forward to my Ed class on Mondays, Wednesdays, and Fridays, or at least to think of it as my favorite part of the day. I didn't skip my readings for it, and I found myself more and more interested in the lectures as the weeks went by.

To my delight, the professor for the course was Dr. Lloyd again. When I registered for classes, I hadn't bothered looking at who the professors were. Getting Dr. Lloyd again was a merciful blessing for the semester.

Dr. Lloyd assigned us a field study mid-semester that was absolutely mandatory. *Field study* was a funny thing to call it, I thought. It made it sound like an archaeological dig. In reality, the field study was more like a student-teaching gig. We would each be assigned an after-school class at a local elementary school to teach over the course of a few sessions.

This actually sounded fun to me. When Dr. Lloyd passed out the course syllabus on the first day of class, I had been a little horrified to see *off-campus field study* as one of the assignments. But teaching kids in an after-school class sounded a lot like summer camp.

I got assigned to an elementary school in Brookline, fourth grade. I'd be teaching them storytelling. I jumped immediately into planning.

When I told Mike about the field study, he was interested, but not very surprised by my reaction.

"You're really into this Ed class, huh?" he said.

"I guess so. I kind of liked my Ed class last semester, too. This one has actually got a lot of interesting theory. Like, I don't hate the readings."

"You may be the first college student who has ever said that."

“I mean it, though,” I insisted. “And Dr. Lloyd is great.”

“You sound like a disciple.” He balled up a sheet of notebook paper and tossed it to me.

“That’s weird. I’m not weird about it, I’m just into it.” I tossed the paper ball back, and he caught it easily.

“Do you even like kids?”

“I don’t know. I’ve never had any.”

“Ha, ha, very funny. Really, though, how do you know you’ll still like it when you actually have to stand in front of the little suckers?”

“I don’t,” I said. “I guess that’s what the field study is for. So, can you look over my lesson plan?”

Mike glanced at his watch. “Actually, our session is technically up.”

“That’s bullshit. You haven’t helped me with anything this whole time. I want my money back.”

“You’re not paying me, the college is. But how about this: I’ll buy us coffee and we can look at your lesson plan off the clock.”

"Deal," I said. "Now?"

"Sure. A little caffeine at night never hurt anyone."

We picked up our notebooks and papers and went down the stairs to the café in the main campus building. There were tables spread in the vast expanse around the coffee bar, and it was invigorating to see so many people sitting there, busy. Each person had their own book or computer or notebook, which meant they each had their own class, which meant they each had their own major and their own trajectory toward something, and that something had brought them to a little table outside a café on a weeknight. It felt like a sacred sisterhood.

"How do you take it?" Mike asked, pulling me out of my reverie.

"One cream, no sugar," I said. "Thanks."

I grabbed one of the empty tables and put my books down, then readied my lesson plan. It was still scribbled on notebook paper, but the first class was a whole week away. Mike came back with the cups of coffee and set one down in front of me. The smell of the coffee, mixed with the bright lights and the student chatter and the pen in my hand, gave me a sudden, intense feeling of, *this is college, this is what I am here for*. The feeling surprised me. I had not had a feeling quite like it since the first time I went to a party in the fall semester.

Mike picked up my lesson plan and started to read it, his brow furrowed slightly in concentration. I sipped my coffee and watched my friend over the cup, and in that moment, I felt quite happy.

The next week, after Ed class got out and I had lunch (alone in the cafeteria, but that was okay), I got on the bus to go to the elementary school in Brookline. Brookline, from what I had heard, was a handful. It was something of a privileged area, and it firmly established itself as "not the same city as Boston." You even needed a different library card to check out books there. From everything I had seen and read about education, this was actually one of the most ideal environments for a school—mostly because of all the money they were willing to throw into it.

The bus pulled up right in front of the elementary school. It was a pristine building, kept nice and tidy right down to the landscaping. I walked through the freshly-Windexed glass doors and found the principal's office to get a visitor's pass.

"Hello," I greeted the secretary. "I'm Kayla, from Simmons College?" I wasn't sure why I made that a question; I was sure that I was, in fact, Kayla from Simmons College. Yet I suddenly found myself nervous.

"Oh, good, you're early," the secretary said. "Here, clip a visitor's pass onto your shirt. I'll take you to the multipurpose room."

She led me down a hallway with walls painted the same pale green that must have been sold at a discount to schools in the 1970s. As school had not been dismissed yet, two straight lines of students passed by us in the hallway. Their mouths hung absently open at the sight of this stranger with the secretary, and their teacher at the front of the lines barked at several of them to face front and watch where they were going.

"Well, this is it," the secretary said when we got to the multipurpose room. "Do you need anything to set up?"

"I'm good, thanks," I told her, and she was gone, leaving me alone with the pleasant-looking, heavyset teacher's aide in the corner. There in the multipurpose room—what a concept for a room, by the way; brilliant with its endless possibilities, and its unapologetic title—I felt another surge of panic. In less than half an hour, this room would be filled with fourth graders who both depended on me and expected me to lead them through a storytelling class. I was in charge, and for the first time, there was no one I could turn to for questions. *I* was that person.

I arranged the chairs in a circle and read over my notes again. The lesson was not complicated. I just had to make it happen.

“Is this storytelling?”

I looked up from the table I had been using as a makeshift desk, and there was a little girl in the doorframe. She literally had a bow tied at the top of her head, which I didn’t know any child but Cindy Lou Who actually did. I gave her a warm smile.

“It sure is. Come on in,” I said. The girl took a seat in the circle, and more of the fourth graders trickled in after her. Before long, the circle was full, and all the students were chattering while they waited for the class to begin.

I realized that I had no idea how to get their attention. People supposedly did this all the time, but I had never been the person in charge, the one to bring everyone to order. *How the hell do I do that?*

“Um, hi,” I tried, which naturally did not work. The kids went right on talking. “Listen up!” I cried. This worked better, but the kids looked up at me in a slightly terrified silence. I would have to work on that one.

“Welcome to storytelling,” I said, softening my voice. “My name is Miss Kayla, and I am excited to work with you over the next few weeks. Now, how many of you have ever told a story before?"

Several of the kids raised their hands. "Good," I said. "For those of you who did not raise your hands, I bet that you *have* told a story, maybe without even realizing it. We tell stories all the time. Any time you tell someone what happened during the day, or recall a memory, you are telling a story. And stories can tell us a whole lot."

To my delight, the students seemed interested. They were quiet and listened to me talk, genuinely engaged with what I had to say. This was a boon.

We went around the circle and all the students said their names, and then I split them into pairs.

"Your assignment," I told them, "is to tell your partner a story. It can be any story at all, and each of you will get a turn. But telling is not the only part of the assignment; the second part is listening."

I gave the students about ten minutes to tell each other stories. This was another strange thing about being the person in charge: I didn't actually have to do the thing I was instructing everyone to do. While they sat and thought and told and listened, all I had to do was listen. That was educational in itself. I heard laughter, sighs, crescendos of voices, clashing punctuation from pair to pair. It was symphonic.

When ten minutes had passed, I tried to get their attention. "Time's up," I called. This proved much more effective than scaring everyone into submission like the last time around. "There is a second part to this assignment," I said. "Your job now is to tell your partner's story, this time to the whole group."

The kids made noises that I had not heard since I was in elementary school myself. "Yessss," some of them hissed, while others sighed, and still others simply ad-libbed their immediate reactions. They all leaned in to listen to the first storytelling volunteer.

And, somehow, it worked. To my amazement, the lesson went off without a hitch. Each of the kids told a story, and they really got into it. Plus, watching them showed me what I could work on for next time. I felt like an actual teacher.

The thing that really got me, though, was listening to one of the girls start describing the class to her mother, who came in to pick her up.

"And then, we had to tell a story," the girl said, "and then *everybody* had to tell *everybody* a story. And actually, I'm telling you a story right now!"

It meant they had listened to me, and *heard.*

Part of the field study assignment was a write-up and reflection for each of the classes we taught at our assigned schools. I may have gushed a little in mine. I was just so impressed with the kids, and so enthralled by the idea of putting all my theory reading to work, that I couldn't help myself. I wrote my first response paper as soon as I got back to my room after the lesson.

Dr. Lloyd graded it the next day and gave me an A. She typed in a comment at the bottom. "It seems more and more that you have a knack for this," she wrote. "Have you thought about an Education major?"

Dr. Lloyd, I wanted to tell her, *I don't think I've considered any major in a real way at all. Are you sure about this knack?* Instead, I wrote an email that said, Dr. Lloyd, could you please tell me more about the Education major?

When I pressed send, I felt like I was finally headed in some sort of direction.

CHAPTER 9

"You're telling me you've never considered an Education major?"

I was in Dr. Lloyd's office and looking at her from across her desk. My chair was awkwardly positioned to face the wall instead of her, and I had been too timid to move it. She had almost certainly done this on purpose.

"I've just never really considered any major. Seriously, I mean," I said.

"I don't mean it to criticize you, really," Dr. Lloyd continued. "I'm just surprised. I've been impressed with your attitude in class, especially this semester, and you seem to know what you're doing."

"Well, I'm trying. I do like it, a lot. And I love the kids in Brookline. So, if I decide to make Education my major, what do I have to do?"

She talked me through a list of requirements before giving me a printout with all of them written out. The whole thing was slightly overwhelming. If I was doing my quick math correctly, an Education major would leave me room for two electives at most. That was a lot of pressure to get it right, to choose the right classes on the first try. And if all I had now in college was my classes, then getting it right was a must.

I brought this up to Dr. Lloyd.

"A lot of people worry about that," she said. "But honestly, it turns out not to be an issue. You're choosing Education for a reason, right? So no matter what classes you choose, you'll already be doing things that interest you."

This was a good point. My gut instinct was to argue, but I stopped myself. Would I be arguing with her reasoning, really, or with my decision to make a decision?

I looked down at the requirements sheet. All those courses on top of the gen eds, plus a capstone at the end. *Capstones in Education Studies are designed to give graduates hands-on experience in a teaching role. During the final semester, students will be assigned fifteen hours per week teaching a class at a local school within the student's chosen grade level*, the paper read. That was a hell of a commitment.

I glanced back up at Dr. Lloyd. Her face was serious and a little stern, but I detected a genuine excitement in her eyes. If she didn't love the idea of me teaching, she at least loved the idea of teaching, and that was enough.

"I'll do it," I said.

Dr. Lloyd's face erupted into a smile, and she congratulated me and shook my hand. I felt like I was graduating already.

She told me to go over to the registrar's office to fill out a form that would officially put my major—on paper and on computers—as Education Studies. When I was finished with that, she directed me, I was to go to the Ed Studies office and fill out a form naming her as my new advisor. I felt like the unexpected winner of college, bumped up from underdog status.

When I was armed with a full to-do list, Dr. Lloyd stood up and extended her arm over the desk. "Kayla," she said, "welcome aboard."

Mike was pleased when I saw him the next night for tutoring and told him about my decision.

"Way to go, kid," he said. "I'm pumped you're so into this teaching thing."

"Thanks," I answered. "I mean, it's not really just a teaching thing. It's a career."

"Yeah, exactly. And remember a couple weeks ago when you didn't have a major, Ms. Career?"

"More like the day before yesterday when I didn't have a major."

He laughed. "What about Calc, though? Unfortunately, that's still a gen ed that you have to finish."

"I know," I sighed. "It's just really terribly un-fun."

"It's not supposed to be fun, it's calculus. How far along are you?"

"I'm in the week-ten problem set now."

"That's not bad, actually. Especially when you've got five classes on top of that." His face turned serious. "I don't think you give yourself enough credit, Kayla. You really do have your shit together."

He looked me deep in the eyes and stretched his arms across the table where we were working, then spread his fingers as if reaching for me. I couldn't figure out what he was trying to do. Up until then, I hadn't thought of Mike as anything but a friend. I didn't want anything else; I wasn't looking for it. In my inconclusive puzzlement, my cheeks flushed. I became suddenly hyper-aware of the silence in the room, the way you notice the silence when a noise cuts out unexpectedly.

"You don't know the half of it, Mike," I said. I scooted my chair back, and it scraped loudly against the tiled floor. Mike winced. "I have to go. There's an Ed department meeting."

This was the truth, and also a good excuse for leaving the tutoring session that had become so uncomfortable all of a sudden. I had been thinking of Mike as my only friend since the beginning of the semester, but now he was just being weird. Could I chalk it up to mid-semester stress, or had he been planning something other than friendship this whole time?

If my new plan worked out, though, then I'd have a much longer list of friends, or at least colleagues. I wasn't sure if I was allowed to think of my classmates as colleagues when I was a just-declared freshman, but I figured it was worth a shot. The plan was to join the Future Teachers of America club. Dr. Lloyd had highly recommended FTA over the course of our advising meeting, and my obsessive preliminary Googling had revealed that Simmons's FTA alumnae were at the top of the field.

I pushed open the doors of the main campus building and started across the quad to the School of Social Work, where FTA met in one of the classrooms. I tried not to associate the School of Social Work with Mike, and instead focused on the arrival of spring in the quad. It was one of the first days of the year that didn't require a jacket to go outside, and those days were my favorite. It made me feel fresh and free, and renewed my desire to know Boston. I silently planned a trip to go walking and exploring the next day.

The room was full when I walked into the second-floor classroom. The desks were arranged in a circle, much the same way as I had arranged them for my storytelling lesson. I wondered if this was a natural teacher instinct.

I took one of the few empty desks near the front of the room. My back was to the whiteboard where the meeting agenda was written, so I swiveled in my chair. All around me, girls were talking in groups and pairs, but I did not pay attention to them. It would come in time, I thought. I read through the agenda and committed it to memory.

After a few minutes, the rest of the desks filled up, and then an energetic girl with a ponytail called the meeting to order.

"Clap once if you can hear me," she said. A few of the girls clapped. Was she serious? "Clap twice if you can hear me," she continued. Most of the girls stopped talking then and clapped twice.

That was one way to call a room to order. I had thought it too condescending even for my fourth-graders, though.

"Alright, welcome to our monthly meeting, everyone," ponytail girl said. "I see we have a newcomer."

I smiled warmly and nodded to her. "Hi, I'm Kayla—" I started, but she cut me off, enormously businesslike.

"We'll do introductions in a minute," she said. "We usually just have new members at the beginning of the semester. But we have a little space, so you'll be fine. Alma? The minutes?"

A pretty girl with a Peter Pan collar stood up and read from her computer. She gave a rundown of the minutes from the last meeting, and I listened politely.

"Thank you, Alma," ponytail girl replied. "Now would be a good time for introductions. My name is Mallory, and I'm the president of FTA. Would the board like to introduce themselves and their positions?"

The girl beside her waved. "Hi, I'm Rubina. I'm vice president."

"I'm Alma. I'm the secretary," said the girl who had read the minutes.

"And I'm Elise, the treasurer," continued a girl from the other side of the room.

Everyone else was silent, which I took as my cue to speak up. "Um, hi. I'm Kayla. I just declared."

Rubina smiled at me. "Welcome to FTA, Kayla."

"If we could, let's get to work now," Mallory said. "We have a lot to do to wrap up the semester."

Wrap up the semester? It was barely April. Was this really considered the end of the semester? And if so, had I just stuttered my way to the end of my freshman year?

I did not open my mouth for the next hour or so, but just listened. FTA was fascinating. Most of the girls were sophomores or upperclassmen. This made me feel out of place, but I supposed most freshmen hadn't declared yet. The club probably didn't even know what to do with me. I wondered if this was what it was like for any freshman to join something.

FTA was planning a fundraiser for May—a bake sale, which people still did, apparently—and a training session for underclassmen in the Ed department. During the planning stages of the training session, I stopped being able to keep my mouth shut.

"But what are we training the underclassmen *for*?" I asked.

Mallory turned to me, visibly annoyed. "Teaching," she said.

"There are a lot of things involved with teaching," I pointed out.

"Well, of course. That's why we'll hire a professional who will figure it out. Like, someone from Northeastern or something."

"Shouldn't we tell them what we want them to focus on, though?"

"This is really something that the upperclassmen are planning," Mallory said. "You can leave it to us. But you can probably attend or help out, okay?"

I sat back in my chair, defeated. There was not a lot that I, a newcomer, could say to the people in charge of the club. I would just have to go along with it.

When the meeting ended, the board and some of the older girls stayed behind, falling in naturally with one another. They planned to go out for burritos after and just hang out post-meeting. I wanted to go with them and meet some of the girls in the club, but no one realized I was still there. They didn't think to invite me.

Later that month, I volunteered to help facilitate the underclassmen training session, hoping to earn my place in FTA. I was happy to do it, since I had plenty of free time. Grace and Christina were still keeping to themselves, or their respective partners, and so my social life remained restricted to Mike. Neither of us mentioned the awkward almost-hand-holding, and we quickly fell back into texting and joking with each other.

The training session was scheduled for a Saturday. Professors in the Ed department had marketed it as "highly recommended," which most underclassmen were still young enough to interpret as mandatory. Because of this, the session roster was full. I felt smugly superior to the girls on the list, for once, thanks to my status as a facilitator.

That is, until the day of the training arrived. It was booked in the big conference room in the main campus building. I arrived early in the morning, fresh and awake after my night of not going out. Mallory and Rubina were already there when I came in.

"We need to put up tables in a circle and set up chairs around them," Mallory said. *Aye aye, captain,* I thought. *Teachers are really into this circle thing, aren't they?*

I kicked rusty table legs into place and dragged the tables across the carpet while Mallory and Rubina hung up big sheets of lined paper around the room. Soon, the room was set up and the woman leading the session arrived. They really had gotten a professor from Northeastern: Dr. Ruby Lowell. She was a good one, too. I had read a paper she had written for my Ed Theory class. When she walked in the door, I actually froze for a few seconds, star-struck.

"Welcome to Simmons, Dr. Lowell," Mallory

announced, striding forward to greet her. "I'm Mallory. We're so glad to have you."

"I'm Rubina. Thank you so much for running the session," Rubina said. They had snapped into perfect professional mode just like that. I was impressed.

"Nice to meet you both," Dr. Lowell said. "I'm excited to be here."

"Kayla, would you sit at the registration table and start checking people in?" Mallory said. It was a command, not a question, which you could do with the upperclassman advantage. I squinted my eyes and frowned, but nodded.

Freshmen and sophomores were already lined up outside the conference room by the registration table. I took my seat behind it and started checking people in, glad that I had a job that was useful and that I couldn't mess up.

The line went quickly, and I was focused. Then, I looked up to greet the next student and found myself face-to-face with Hannah, a girl from Shruti's crew that I hadn't seen since the fall. At first, her face blanched as much as I imagined my face was blanching, and then she smirked.

"Hey, Kayla," she said. "I haven't seen you all semester. What have you been up to? Running the little teachers' club?"

"Um, I didn't know you were an Ed major," I answered quietly.

"Oh, I'm undeclared. Just leaving my options open."

"Well—"

"It's too bad you're out here and can't come to training. I'm sure you could use it." With that, she took her registration packet, slapped on a nametag, and strutted into the conference room. Somehow, even though we were on carpet, her heels *clack-clacked* against the floor to announce her arrival.

For my part, I was a little confused. First of all, Hannah did not have much room to talk about who needed teacher training—I resented that. And second, I had never known Hannah well or even seen her outside those wild fall parties, but it was not hard to see the girl she was. Or, for that matter, to imagine the sort of girl she wanted to be—the sort she had been preparing to be all year long. From what I could tell, that girl was *not* one that cared deeply about education, either her own or as a general concept. The poison in her voice must have been a product of pure one-upmanship.

I shook off Hannah and checked in the rest of the line. Then, I collected the extra papers and nametags and took a seat at the back of the room to listen to the presentation.

Watching it was jarring. For one thing, Dr. Ruby Lowell was brilliant. Listening to her theories of education was invigorating; I felt half-geek and half-scholar. I was almost glad that Mallory and the board hadn't taken my advice and given her a topic to focus on, since that meant she could focus on whatever she wanted. People in academia, I was learning, loved to talk uninterrupted about the things that really fired them up.

But it was also jarring to watch the freshmen and sophomores who were attending the training. They sat in groups at the tables I had set up, and they all seemed to know each other already. They chatted and laughed as they did the group activities together, and from my spot at the back of the room, I could see them whispering to each other and exchanging glances all throughout the presentation.

What had I done wrong? I thought declaring my major and joining FTA would bring me together with people who shared my same new interest. But I realized, sickeningly, that I still had not actually tried to talk to anybody. I just couldn't meet these strangers, even if they were supposed to be my colleagues.

I was surprised to find my cheeks getting hot and my breath growing short. My eyes began to strain and sting. After everything, I couldn't take this last exclusion.

I went up to Mallory, sitting in the far corner of the room, and tapped her on the shoulder. "I have to go," I said in a small voice. "I'm not feeling well."

Mallory frowned. “Oh, you don’t look so good. Go home and get some rest, you must be stressed out.” I nodded. Then she added, “By the way, Kayla, I’m sorry if I snapped at you. I guess I’m stressed, too, with my capstone and everything. But we’re happy to have you here, really.”

I smiled at this, surprised and not quite sure what to make of it. *She’s a human being, Kayla,* said a voice in my head. *Remember that? She’s not perfect.* I felt a little better, and I walked home with, if nothing else, a fresher appreciation of my new club and its president.

CHAPTER 10

April faded into the dust as I spent more and more time on my Ed class and tried to carve out a space for myself in the department. It felt pathetic to cling only to my newfound department as a young college student, but I was stranded. I didn't have any other options.

Mike was encouraging about it. He had started doing more and more sessions with me off the clock, which often just turned into study parties in the group study rooms at the library. This made me a little uneasy since I was still unsure whether he was trying to push things in a romantic direction, but I made sure to keep things strictly platonic. He was starting to think about his dissertation, and we listened to each other wax poetic and idealistic about the obscure topics we really cared about. He was trying to change gears and write about teenagers for his dissertation, and I was fascinated by some of the stories he told me about teens and behavior disorders. It actually tied nicely to my Education major, and we got into spirited discussions.

Anyone else would have called us geeks.

Since Ed Theory and Practice was not a class I had to really push myself to do, I took to using our tutoring sessions and study parties to work on Calc. By May, I was almost done. The week-thirteen problem set was nearly finished, and I had emailed my professor—really just a grad student in the Math department—to schedule a time to take the exam.

I was almost done with my other classes, too. Finals would be at the end of the month, and I was clipping along at a rate that was perfectly acceptable. It still amazed me how easy it was to get things done for class when I had nothing else to focus on. I could even understand what my professor was saying in French class. I was lonely, yes, but at least with this sort of loneliness, I wasn't picking one friend group over another and worrying what the rejected group thought. It was perversely comforting to be the one who was rejected.

I brought it up to Mike one night when we were in the library. "You spend virtually all your time on Social Work stuff," I said. "And tutoring, too, I guess, since that's your job. Don't you ever feel kind of lonely?"

Mike laughed. "I don't really think grad school is for making friends," he said. "Everyone in my program really just focuses on work."

"But undergrad wasn't like that, was it?"

"No, undergrad wasn't like that."

"What am I doing wrong, then?" I sighed. "I'm focusing on my work, sure, but I haven't got anybody. And I can't even meet people in the Ed department, which is about the only thing that matters to me right now."

"You've got me," he reminded me. His eyes were somber for a moment, and then he shook his head. "Plus, it would be totally abnormal for you to know everyone in the Ed department right now. You're still a freshman, and you only just declared."

"Most freshmen Ed majors seem to all know each other."

"Half the Ed majors who graduate the same year as you won't even declare until next spring," Mike shot back. "And how many other freshmen are in FTA? I think you're ahead of the game, Kayla. You're too hard on yourself."

"Mike, how did you pick Social Work in the first place? If you're doing concerts and stuff like the one you did with Shruti, how come that's not what you study? How come you don't hang out with those people?"

"Everything is not always clear cut," he replied. "Some things are hobbies. Some things I just enjoy. Other things are career related."

He paused, shut his mouth, then opened it again.

He looked at me meaningfully. "It's not always clear to me what I want, Kayla."

"What does that mean?"

"I don't know. It's just . . . I think you'll find that as college moves along, things won't be as neat or clear as you want them to be."

"I don't get it. I'm just trying to make friends and balance that out with school."

Mike looked like he wanted to say something, but he couldn't seem to form a word. *Oh gosh, please don't let him try to turn this into something other than friendship*, I thought. *Why can't I just have one friend?* He leaned forward then and looked me square in the eye.

"I, um, should go. I have a meeting," I said, before he could say anything. I closed my Calc book and slipped it into my bag. Mike watched me, but I couldn't read his face. I was out the door before he could think about protesting.

The next day was my last storytelling class in Brookline. I refused to think about the Mike business and put it out of my mind. Instead, I dressed up elaborately for the last class and put on earrings that jingled when I walked. I even made peanut butter brownies in Bigelow's tiny kitchen for all the students.

My lesson plan for the day was to have the students retell classic fairytales set in the modern world. It would be a fun way to end things, I thought, and it would be congenial to sit around, munching brownies, and telling each other fairytales. The kids would love it.

I got off the bus at the elementary school, and the secretary smiled at me when I came in. She knew me by now, and she was pleased with how much the students loved the storytelling class. When she handed me my visitor's pass and I smiled back at her—I felt genuinely at home there.

The multipurpose room felt like home, too, especially once I pulled the chairs into our customary circle. I laid out the brownies on the table and started drawing pictures of castles and fairies and centaurs on the dry-erase whiteboard. Soon, the students starting filtering in and joining me at the board, adding their own drawings.

When the room was full, I asked the students to take their seats.

"Who can guess what we are doing today?" I asked when they were all seated. One boy raised his hand.

"Fairytales!" he shouted. It was much more of a statement than a guess, and I smiled.

"Right! But not just any fairytales. Today, you get to choose any fairytale you'd like to tell to the class, but with one catch. You'll have to tell the story as if it takes place today, in the modern world."

The students squirmed with excitement. I beamed, pleased that the plan would be fun for them.

"Plus," I added, "as an extra special treat for our last class, we have brownies today! As you come get them, start thinking about your fairytales."

The students hissed the familiar "*Yesssss,*" and then filed up to grab brownies. When they were all grinning and back in their seats, I asked for a volunteer to tell the first fairytale. Many of them raised their hands—an improvement from the first class, when I'd had to push them a little to get going.

"Lily, why don't you start?" I said, choosing one of the girls. She sat up straight in her chair and readied herself for a dramatic retelling of Little Red Riding Hood set in the mean streets of L.A.

Then, one of the boys started to cough. Lily paused to wait for him to finish, so as not to be drowned out, but the coughing continued. And continued. My heart racing, I looked toward the boy and saw that his eyes were bulging. He couldn't stop coughing, and his face was an unnatural shade of red.

"Quick! Please! Someone get the nurse," I shouted. One of the students bolted up and sprinted toward the nurse's office.

When she arrived, the nurse took one look at

the coughing boy and, quick as a flash, she pulled an instrument out of her pocket—some kind of a syringe—and jabbed it into the boy. In seconds, the coughing subsided, and he gasped to catch his breath.

"Take this," the nurse said, handing the boy a tiny pink pill. The nurse got him a cup of water from the sink and watched the boy swallow the pill. Then, she glanced around at the wide-eyed children, who were in shock at seeing this horrific attack in their classmate. That is when she saw the brownies.

"Did someone give him brownies? Do those have peanut butter?" she asked.

"Um, I made brownies. It's our last class," I said.

The nurse shook her head and sighed.

"Tim is allergic to peanuts," the nurse said matter-of-factly, gesturing toward the poor boy, whose face and neck had swelled up like a balloon. "I'm certain the principal and Tim's parents will have more to say to you."

I gaped at her, dumbfounded, and shocked at myself. This was it. My last class, the one thing I had felt really good at, was over, and I had messed it up in an instant. Not just messed it up, but really, horribly destroyed it. There went my role as a teacher, as someone who cared about her students. It was the teacher's job to think of everything, to keep these sorts of things from happening. There went any chance of actually having a direction to steer my life. And all because I was trying to do something good.

The nurse led Tim out of the room, stopping at the door to shake her head one last time at me. "Let's go call your parents," she said to Tim.

I let the students have free time for the remainder of the class and busied myself with cleaning the room. One by one, their parents came to pick them up, and the students left in an embarrassed silence.

I shut off all the lights before I left. I felt like the punch line of the joke that was my own life.

When I got back to my room, I threw the door open with such force that Grace was alarmed. She spoke to me for maybe the first time that week.

"You okay?" she asked.

"Yeah. Sorry. Pissed off," I answered. I wanted her to ask what was wrong. I wanted her to let me come back and talk to her and be her friend again, to have one thing to hold on to. I wanted to feel welcome and at home in my room, to undo everything I had done since the stupid Columbus Day weekend party I had insisted on going to.

If only I could go back to that Saturday night and just watch *The Office* with my roommate.

But Grace just nodded and put her headphones on.

I started ransacking my closet for something to wear. It was a Thursday night, which meant people would be out somewhere. Thirsty Thursday—that was a thing I definitely remembered from the fall semester. Toward the back of my closet, I found a jean skirt. I threw it on, then shaved my legs dry. I nicked my knee, so I spat on my finger and rubbed out the blood. All the while, I tried to push the thoughts of that afternoon out of my head. The mental picture of the little boy choking felt branded on my brain.

The old handle of vodka was still under my bed. I pulled it out and dusted it off, squinting to see how much was in the bottle. Enough, I thought. I took a swig. Following this up with a few coats of mascara, I started to feel good.

"I'm going out," I announced, but Grace didn't hear me.

The night air was the comfortable cool of late spring that warned of summer. I closed my eyes in the dark beauty of it and took a deep breath. The campus air smelled like peonies and my vodka.

I walked through the campus and the surrounding streets, with no destination in mind, but listening for the first hint of a party that might appear. I entered, without knocking, the first house that had the sounds of screeching guitars and laughter wafting out the windows. The party inside was dark and dank, just as I wanted.

Kitchens, as I remembered from my experience the previous semester, were easy to find at these kinds of parties, and that's where the booze always was. I slipped into the kitchen and found a nearly full bottle of rum. Perfect.

There was an impossibly tall boy leaning against the kitchen counter. He watched as I poured the rum into a red plastic cup.

"Tough day?" he asked.

I took a dainty sip. "I guess," I said.

He leaned back on his elbows. "It's kind of that time of the semester. I haven't seen you around, are you at Northeastern?"

"No," I said, "Simmons." I took a bigger gulp of the rum. Then another. It tingled on my tongue, and I realized I missed it.

"Nice. So, what brings you here?" he asked.

I grinned. "The tough day."

"Maybe I can make it a little less tough for you."

I finished the drink. Poured another.

He led me to one of the dark rooms with lots of low couches, and his lips were on mine immediately. My head, my body swam around him. The heat of his chest radiated against me, and I felt his teeth on my neck. I felt like I was falling deep, deep.

"Kayla."

I pulled back. "Um, did I tell you my name?"

"Kayla," I heard again. His mouth didn't move. Then, I felt a hand on my shoulder.

Mike was standing there, drink in hand.

"Kayla, what are you doing?" he said. The boy underneath me took this as a cue and wriggled away.

"What the hell?" I said. My speech slurred and I tripped over the words. How much had I had to drink? "What are you doing?"

"No, that's what I just asked you. God, fix your shirt."

I hastily tried to make my hands work and pull my top up. It had slipped down over my bra, and he was staring at it.

"Why can't you mind your own fucking business, Mike?" I grabbed his wrist—it took two tries—and looked him in the eye. "Why can't you accept that I'm not your damn girlfriend, and let me do what I want?"

Even with my head swimming, I could see the hurt in his eyes. He grabbed my wrist with his free hand and just held it there. We looked like we were in some kind of ridiculous miniature circus grab. I was terrified that he would bend down and just kiss me right there. And there was a tiny part of me that wanted him to.

Finally, he shook his head and let go.

"Fuck it. Go home, Kayla."

And I did. I couldn't see anything on the solo walk to my dorm. My eyes were blurred with tears and liquor. I stumbled and couldn't see what I stumbled on, and when I finally stuck my key in the door, I nearly snapped it in the lock.

Grace had been sleeping, but she bolted awake when the door opened with a bang. And she saw me in the doorframe, glowing in the dim hall light, my hand on my chin to wipe off a dribble of spit.

"I'm not calling an ambulance on you again," Grace said.

That's when I started to cry. I fell to my knees

in the doorway and sobbed. Sighing, yet ever herself, Grace rose from her bed and gently shushed me. She pulled me into the room, tucked me into bed, and made me drink water. And she let me cry. For a length of time I couldn't possibly measure, she held my hand. She held it until I fell asleep.

CHAPTER 11

Somehow, I got through the minor scolding from the Brookline School principal (which included a number of instances of her saying, "Sometimes it's just best not to feed children in school") and made it to finals.

Classes ended without fanfare, and we all adjusted to the quiet solitude of finals. For me, blessedly, it wasn't true solitude anymore. I had Grace back.

She hadn't made it easy to return to what we had been, but I didn't blame her. I deserved it.

The morning after the terrible run-in with Mike, she said that we should talk, and so I followed her to the cafeteria for breakfast. I pushed my scrambled eggs around on my plate while I waited for her to speak.

"So. You didn't black out last night," she finally started.

"Yeah."

"That's an improvement on last time."

"I don't get it. Were you there?"

"I called the ambulance on you, Kayla," she said. "I told you that last night."

"Seriously? That was actually you?"

"Yeah, of course it was. I mean, you came back and just completely collapsed. I didn't know what else to do." She paused and looked down at her plate. "I didn't know everything that would happen, you know. I was just freaked out. *You* really freaked me out. So I stayed up all night to make sure you were okay."

"You did?"

"Yeah. I mean, I only left to go to my final."

I didn't deserve to benefit from how good Grace was.

So, she slowly let me back into the warmth of her friendship, and we were all right with one another by finals. She didn't even mind if I drank, she told me, she just didn't want to see her roommate passed out and unresponsive on the floor again.

I didn't blame her.

That finals period, we re-christened the Grace-Christina-Kayla table in the library. I was glad to see Christina join us. It turned out that she had been thoroughly depressed all spring, and had barely seen Grace at all. That made me feel even worse. It meant Grace had gone through the whole semester without either one of her best friends.

But we used finals period to try to come back together. Grace brought Gao to our study table, and Christina brought her girlfriend, Maddy. I could have brought Mike, I guess, but I was still hurt by the feeling that he wasn't really looking at me as a friend, but as someone he could have. I couldn't quite put my finger on what had made me so mad about him interfering at the party, but my independence felt totally undermined. I was ready to leave that, at least, behind, before I tried to sort out my feelings.

Plus, we were not even really talking. When I didn't show up for our first tutoring session after the party, he had texted me, Coming?, and I'd told him no, not tonight, and that I needed to think about things. And I hadn't heard from him since. Neither of us was ready.

Late in May, I went to my Calc professor's tiny office to take my final exam. "Just do what you can," she said. "I've seen your problem sets, and I think you'll be okay." I gave her a grateful smile. She didn't want me to fail, I knew. And I had worked hard enough all semester that I was ready to put my all into the exam.

That final led into all the rest. In the library with my friends, I toiled away, eager to prove to them that I belonged there, that I was worthwhile. We were all a little tense at first, but we eased into our old rapport. I started to wonder why, and certainly regret, that I had ever considered Grace and Christina too uninteresting for my purposes—but I supposed it was about time to stop judging the people I was trying to be friends with. Maybe Grace and Christina—just like Annie and Liz, whom I could try to go back to—were the kind of friends I'd been longing for. They were the forever kinds of characters in my own story.

The assignments got checked off the list one by one: Business Management paper. Bio exam. French oral. English paper. Then, finally, a write-up of my Ed Studies field study, complete with an analysis and quotes from Northeastern's Dr. Ruby Lowell. Sitting at the library table with my friends, a giant bag of M&Ms on the table between us, and cups of coffee everywhere, I didn't hate it.

After I turned in my last final, I had my meeting with Dean Storey. Waiting outside her office in the main campus building was less scary this time. I didn't feel great, but I had done the semester. It had happened. Now, all I had to do was tell her so.

I knocked on the door, and she called, "Come in." She was sitting at her desk this time, not the round table, and there were no other unexpected guests in the office. As happy as I had been to have Dr. Lloyd's contributions last time around, I was relieved at this.

Dean Storey had her glasses on top of her head and a pile of papers in her hand. She looked dreadfully busy, and instead of feeling afraid of her, I was sorry for bothering her.

"Have a seat, Miss Howard," she said. I did. "You've made it through the semester without incident, I see."

On her desk, my file was open. I was suddenly curious about these files. Where were they stored and what usually went in them when someone hadn't completely destroyed their freshman year?

Were they just empty? Mine had a piece of paper with a thick black stripe down the middle.

"Yes, I made it through," I said. Saying it out loud felt good. More than good. It felt like an entire weight, like a pile of boulders had been lifted off me. I had made it through. I had made it through the semester and my freshman year and the feeling of having no idea whatsoever about my life's direction. Maybe I'd even be able to earn back my respect as a future teacher. Maybe my parents wouldn't be disappointed in my failure to know or do anything for sure. Maybe, too, I could stop being disappointed in myself.

"And your incomplete from the fall?" Dean Storey asked.

"I passed," I told her. It was true. My Calc professor had sent me my exam back a week before through campus mail. I got an A-minus, and she even drew a smiley face on it. *Suck it, integrals.*

Dean Storey pulled her glasses down onto her face, and she scanned through my file. "Your professors have given you glowing remarks this semester, particularly Dr. Lloyd in the Education Department. She tells me you declared an Education major."

I nodded. "I really loved Dr. Lloyd's class," I said. "And I taught a short fourth-grade course this semester, which I enjoyed so much." I didn't mention Tim and his allergic reaction. But she did.

"Yes. I did hear about that project. A child named Tim . . . "

Immediately, my face flushed and I looked down at my lap.

"That was a huge mistake, Dean Storey. It's something I'm ashamed of, and something I will never let happen again." Then, with a flicker of determination, I lifted my eyes to meet hers. "This is all too important to me to let go of it now. I *need* to be a teacher."

She flipped a page and scanned her eyes over the document, then flipped another.

"It seems, Miss Howard," she said, "that this fall

semester was a hiccup. You appear to have turned over a new leaf for the spring." Her face softened suddenly and looked almost motherly. "It can be a difficult task to adjust to college, Kayla. I know that. But bear in mind that the way you end your freshman year means much more than how you began it."

With that, she turned back a few pages in my file to the sheet with the black mark on it. She lifted it out of the file, tore it into four neat strips, and tossed them into the recycling bin.

"How about we start fresh?" she said. My face broke into a smile, and it was a genuine one. I felt that my entire year had been full of firsts, and here was another one: the first time at Simmons that I truly felt someone was on my side. It was a good feeling, and one that I hadn't known I needed so desperately.

"Thank you so much, Dean Storey," I said, rising from my chair and sticking out my hand to shake. "Really, thank you, thank you." I felt like an insincere businessman or a sincere lottery winner. I shook Dean Storey's hand with such ferocity that I imagined she might have had to get the bones set afterward.

With finals over and the year finally winding down, I had one last job: to pack up my room. This was a job Grace and I planned to do together, with the help of pizza and boy band music. Planning it out with Grace almost made it seem fun.

When I got back to our room, there was an entire pizza waiting on top of our fridge, and Grace was standing on her bed and taking posters down. She turned an anxious face toward me when I came in.

"How did it go?" she asked. I hadn't told her everything about the repercussions of my fall semester, but she knew that a bad meeting with the dean might spell disaster for the rest of my college career.

"Really well, actually," I said. "I always kind of thought that deans and people like that liked you to get in trouble, but I think maybe it bums them out just as much as us."

"That's great!" she cried. She jumped off the bed and gave me a big hug. "Let's celebrate," she said. She pulled a bottle out from her closet.

"Champagne?" I asked, puzzled.

"It's really cheap stuff, and Gao got it for me. Now's as good a time as any."

"I didn't know you drank," I admitted.

"There's a way to drink socially and not pass out every weekend."

I deserved that. She popped the cork and poured the champagne into two paper cups we had stolen from the bathroom. Handing one to me, she lifted the other, and cleared her throat.

"Here's to freshman year," she said.

"Here's to roommates who don't hate their friend forever for being an asshole," I added.

"Here's to friends who get better."

We each took a sip, then laughed. As we grabbed pizza and got down to work folding clothes, emptying drawers, and taping boxes, I got serious for just a moment.

"Grace, I really am sorry about what I did all fall," I said. "And spring, too. You know, I didn't even try to fix things. I just went right into my work and forgot everything else."

"From what I hear, freshman year isn't supposed to be easy. Or simple. Or smooth. Or even necessarily healthy," Grace answered.

"Most people manage not to screw it up as royally as I did, though. And I'm never really going to get to do it over."

Grace looked up from the box she was filling and held her hands still. "That's kind of the nature of screwing up, though, isn't it? The point isn't to do it again. It's to be able to do sophomore year, and do it better."

"Grace, you're really something, do you know that?"

She laughed. "That's just because you didn't see everything I screwed up this year. I'm a good hider."

We finished packing up our room that afternoon. Right before we closed our door for the last time, my phone buzzed. It was Mike.

MIKE (2:05pm): Have a good summer, Kayla. I'll miss you.

I bit my lip, unsure what to say. There was a part of me that loved Mike for everything he had been to me for most of the semester. But there was a bigger part that didn't feel ready to trust him completely, not yet. I took a breath and wrote back.

KAYLA (2:07pm): You have a good summer, too. Hopefully see you in the fall?
MIKE (2:08pm): Yeah. Yeah.

And I smiled, because maybe things weren't totally over.

Grace was going back to California for the summer, and so she sent most of her boxes to campus storage. I fit most of my things into small boxes to mail home and stuffed the rest into suitcases. I rolled them along as Grace and I walked to Residential Life to turn in our keys. Passing the envelope with both our keys to the frazzled-looking woman at the counter was simultaneously freeing and tragic. It felt a little like dropping my baby off a cliff.

But Grace was right. Freshman year was over now, and it was something to let go of. I couldn't do it over. And, I realized, I didn't want to. All I could do was move on to sophomore year.

I walked with Grace to the cab she would take to the airport. She looked at peace, and while I wanted to know more about what trials she had gone through without me knowing all year, I knew I had to let her go.

"You'll be on Facebook all summer, right? I'll be able to talk to you?" I asked.

"Of course."

I smiled and squeezed her hand. "Grace," I said. "Enjoy the summer, okay? And I'll see you next year?"

"Always."